"What's the matter, Sid? Don't you trust me?" Gary asked defensively.

"Sure I trust you. It's just that . . ." How could Sid explain to Gary that this deal—the deal that Gary had been working on for weeks—seemed a bit shady? "You can never be too careful, that's all." What if Gary's once-in-a-lifetime deal backfired in their faces? Sid gave a resigned shrug. The deed was already done. Now only time would tell.

_____

Series Story Editor **Mary Ann Cooper** is America's foremost soap opera expert. She writes the nationally syndicated column _Speaking of Soaps_, is a major contributor to soap opera magazines, and has appeared on numerous radio and television talk shows.

Award-winning novelist **Victoria Dann** comes from a family of talented authors. She currently resides on the west coast, where she is a successful screen writer.

Dear Friend,

Pioneer Communications Network takes great pride in presenting the eighth book in the Soaps & Serials paperback series. If this is your first Soaps & Serials book, you're in for a pleasant surprise. Our books give you a glimpse into the past, featuring some of the most exciting stories in the history of television soaps. For those of you who are old friends of the Soaps & Serials line, thanks for your support.

Here's one of the many questions we've received from our thoughtful and loyal fans. A reader from Cheyenne, Wyoming, is convinced that he saw Don Murray's name listed as the writer of an episode of KNOTS LANDING. His wife thinks he's wrong. Is he? If this reader was watching a rerun of KNOTS LANDING, he did not imagine what he saw. Don Murray, who starred as Sid Fairgate in the series, wrote a special two-part episode of KNOTS LANDING entitled "Hitchhiker," which dealt with the Fairgates' problems clearing Sid of charges made by a young woman to whom he offered a ride.

Although we can't answer all of the letters we receive, we still enjoy hearing from you. Keep writing!

For Soaps & Serials Books,

Mary Ann Cooper

Mary Ann Cooper

P.S. If you missed previous Soaps & Serials books and can't find them in your local book source, please see the order form inserted in this book.

KNOTS LANDING™

8

Once in a Lifetime

From the television series created by David Jacobs

PIONEER COMMUNICATIONS NETWORK, INC.

Once in a Lifetime

From the television series KNOTS LANDING™ created by David Jacobs. This book is based on scripts written by Tim Maschler and John Pleshette.

KNOTS LANDING™ paperback novels are published and distributed by Pioneer Communications Network, Inc.

SOAPS & SERIALS™ is a trademark of Pioneer Communications Network, Inc.

ISBN: 0-916217-68-X

Printed in Canada

10 9 8 7 6 5 4 3 2 1

Once in a Lifetime

Chapter One

The Morning Rush

The sun rises in the east, a fact that Californians have always accepted as the small price to pay for spectacular western sunsets. To Karen Fairgate, there was nothing more beautiful than watching the beautiful red-gold orb descend into the Pacific Ocean. Sometimes, she'd take the car and drive to the beach alone, and just sit there, watching the sun go down. The effect it had on her was always the same. She'd feel alive, rejuvenated, ready to conquer the world.

Not that she had anything to be unhappy about. Karen thought about Sid and the kids. All things considered, life had been kind to her. She paused over her morning coffee to reflect upon her neighbors and their complicated lives. Yes, she was luckier than most.

But she had this thing about sunsets,

mainly because she was a night person. She was definitely not a morning person— she had never been one. But when you have three junior Fairgates rushing off to school and a husband who insists on being the first one in the office, you learn to sacrifice a few extra hours of sleep . . . as well as a few sunsets. In addition, her kitchen had become Grand Central Station recently. It was almost a ritual for Val Ewing to stop over for coffee on her way to school. Not that Karen minded Val's company. Val was a gentle-spoken woman, a bit timid. There were still a few mysteries about Valene Ewing that Karen hadn't figured out. But she would, one day.

On this particular morning, Karen was attempting to be productive. Eight A.M. seemed like the perfect time to hang a framed print on the kitchen wall. At the same moment, she was trying to carry on a conversation with Val. Out of the corner of her eye, she observed her friend sitting demurely at the table, drinking coffee and studying class notes. Karen shook her head in amazement. She had to hand it to Val, who was going back to school after all these years.

"And the professors, they're so young," her pretty blond neighbor said, chattering on. "I can't believe how young they are."

Karen looked away from her poster to say sarcastically, "It's the young ones you've got to watch out for, kiddo."

Val sighed. "Do you realize I'm taking classes with students my daughter's age? I mean, that's okay, but some of those teachers . . . well, they're so young I feel like an old lady."

"Maybe you should start wearing bobby socks," Karen said and laughed. Then she stopped. My Lord, Val *was* wearing bobby socks! Karen hoped she hadn't inadvertently hurt the other woman's feelings, but Val blithely rambled on.

"That doesn't mean I don't enjoy classes. I must admit, my favorite is American lit. We're doing *Moby Dick* by Herman Melville." Val paused. "Ever read *Moby Dick*, Karen? It's really interesting."

Karen's attention was on the poster and at exactly what level to hang it. It wasn't her idea of a great objet d'art. The frame was worth more than the print display of culinary herbs. But what could she do? It had been a gift from another neighbor, Laura Avery. She couldn't afford to offend her by not hanging it up.

"It's about a whale, Karen."

"Huh?" was the vague reply.

It was Val's turn to smile. "*Moby Dick*." Sometimes, she couldn't resist the urge to show off her increasing knowledge. Picking up her education where she had left off so many years ago meant everything to Val. She envied all those women with college educations. She wanted to be more than just a sweet but dumb country girl.

Suddenly, her mind was flooded with a bitter memory. J.R. Ewing, her ruthless, sharp-tongued brother-in-law, had used these very words to describe her all those years ago. No, that wasn't quite right. What J.R., that snake in the grass, had actually said was "Valene, honey, you're just a cute but dumb little country girl." He'd been grinning from ear to ear when he'd said it, too. She remembered so clearly how J.R. almost seemed to savor making her feel uncomfortable.

And something else, too, although she'd never mentioned it to anybody, especially Gary. The way J.R. used to taunt her belied something just below the surface. There was always a subtle invitation lurking right beneath his words. Oh, her brother-in-law had never come right out and propositioned her. Not exactly. J.R. was not a man to accept female rejection, he simply wasn't built that way. He was too full of himself. So he never directly asked any woman to sleep with him, not that Val could recall. But she had watched him in action many times. He would send out signals—good Lord, did that man send out signals. And if his target was interested, she would return the signal. Before J.R. had married Sue Ellen, his exploits had been the talk of Texas. And afterward, well . . .

Valene gave another sigh. She'd always

felt a pang of sympathy for any woman who had the misfortune to fall in love with J.R. Ewing. J.R., Bobby, Jock. All the Ewing men had been such heartbreakers. Gary, she thought—oh, Gary. It was so good to be back with her husband after a devastating seventeen-year separation. Although he was a Ewing by blood, there was something that kept him apart, different. Oh, he tried to be ambitious and ruthless like J.R. sometimes, but it never quite worked, because Gary had a conscience. Despite his ambition, Gary lacked the killer instinct. He simply didn't know how to go for the jugular like his brothers could. Maybe that was the reason Gary had never been the success he wanted to be. On the other hand, it was his soft heart that Valene loved. Without his weaknesses he wouldn't be Gary.

"You ready to go, honey?"

A familiar voice interrupted her thoughts. Gary stood in the entrance of the Fairgate kitchen, briefcase in hand. He looked so devastatingly handsome in a tie and sports jacket. Val was flooded with a warm glow. Every time she saw her husband, she fell in love with him all over again. Gary was *her* weakness. He was her Achilles' heel. She could take anything the world dished out, but Gary was her vulnerability.

Gary Ewing smiled at the two women. "Hi, Karen. Tell me, is Sid around?"

Karen was still concentrating on hanging the picture. "What do you think, guys? Does this look straight to you?"

"Too low," Gary said.

"That's because you're too tall," Karen tossed back.

Gary looked around the room restlessly. "Is Sid upstairs?"

Karen put her hands on her hips. What on earth did Gary mean, "Too low." The print was at just the right height. Suddenly aware that Gary was still waiting for an answer, she tore her eyes from the poster and said, "Sid left an hour ago."

"Are you kidding?"

"No. It's too early in the morning to be kidding." For the first time, she noticed how uneasy Val's husband looked. What was eating him this morning? she wondered. Gary Ewing was a nice enough man, but Karen's unerring instinct told her there was a lot going on inside that attractive blond head of his.

Whoops, had she actually admitted he was attractive? Karen suppressed a puckish smile. Well, why not? Just because she was married to Sid Fairgate, the most adorable, wonderful man on earth, didn't mean she couldn't occasionally take a moment to stop and appreciate other men. Gary Ewing's chiseled good looks were attractive in a classic way. In fact, there were many attractive men in Knots Landing.

Of course, this was all from an aesthetic point of view. When it came to anything else, there was something special about Sid. He made any other man seem shallow by comparison. Perhaps it was his integrity. Perhaps it was because his dreams were still intact after all these years. After all the awful things that had happened to him . . . all the rotten turns of luck. She hoped those hard times were all past him now. Of course, she wasn't too optimistic about Sid's appointment with the patent lawyer this morning. Karen couldn't help not being as enthusiastic as her husband. She wasn't a dreamer. She had always been more practical and realistic.

''I thought he'd still be here.'' Gary seemed dejected.

What was he so nervous about? Karen wondered. ''Sid had a nine o'clock appointment with a patent attorney downtown.''

''Patent attorney?'' Gary was genuinely surprised.

''About his engine,'' Karen answered. ''He was really excited. It took him six weeks to set up the appointment.''

Gary gave an impatient sigh. ''We've got a ten o'clock meeting about a possible fleet deal. He's never going to make it.''

''What fleet deal?''

''Orchid Cab and Delivery.'' Gary tapped his fingers on the counter. ''You think he forgot?''

Karen shrugged. "It looks that way." Honestly, what did Gary expect? Sure, as Sid's new business partner, he had all sorts of plans for Knots Landing Motors. But didn't he understand that the most important thing in Sid's life right now was his new engine? The dealership was business, but developing and perfecting that engine was the dream of his lifetime.

"Oh, great. Do you know where to reach him?" Gary persisted.

"I can't remember the lawyer's name—" Karen scratched her head thoughtfully "—but I suppose he might have written it on a piece of paper upstairs."

Gary exhaled. "If you find it, will you give me a call at the office? I'll call the guys and see if they can come in after lunch."

Karen looked at him in wonder. "You know how he is about that engine. Sid was up all night going over his notes." *Please, God*, she prayed silently, *don't make Sid face another disappointment. If he's going to be let down again, let it be gently.*

Gary touched Val affectionately on the shoulder. "Let's go, honey. You can drop me at work and keep the car."

Val gave Karen a wistful wave as she left the house with Gary. Karen watched them go in silence, lost deep in thought. Her conscience was nagging her as she fumbled with a folded piece of paper resting in the bottom of her bathrobe pocket. Should

14

she or shouldn't she? Written on the paper, which Sid had given her before leaving the house this morning, was the phone number of the patent lawyer. She sighed. Perhaps she was being overprotective; after all, Sid could take care of himself. It's just that she hated to have him disturbed this morning of all mornings.

Through the window, Karen watched Gary and Val getting into their car. Another pang of conscience pulled at her. In another moment, Karen rushed to the door and ran out onto the lawn.

"Gary! Wait! I found the number!" she called after them. But it was too late. Her voice was drowned out by the noise of the engine. Karen darted toward the driveway. "Wait a second!" she called out again. But it was futile. The Ewing car had already disappeared down the street. Oh, well. Maybe it was for the best. Karen began walking back toward the house, pausing at a familiar object lying on the grass. It was one of Michael's sneakers. So, what else was new? She smiled to herself as she picked up her son's shoe. Inside the house or out, it seemed she was forever picking up after everybody.

Abby Cunningham stood in front of her bedroom mirror putting the finishing touches on her makeup. She was pleased at the reflection staring back at her. Shiny blond hair, ever so slightly styled on the wild side. The expensive lipstick on her deliberately pouting lips was just the perfect shade of frosted pink. She gave a final check to her eye shadow and was unable to find a single flaw in its application. How many men had told her, with revealing quivers in their voices, just how beautiful her eyes were? Limpid pools, one man had said once.

Abby was coldly realistic about being a beautiful woman. She despised those phony women who pretended to be modest. Abby knew she was beautiful and did everything she could to remind people just how stunning she was. She had always been beautiful. She'd been a beautiful, golden-haired child. When she was a teenager, there was hardly a man who didn't try to get what he could from her. She remembered more than one teacher asking her to stay after school for some extra "tutoring." Ha! It was then she decided most men were out for what they could get. The only thing that mattered to her was to survive, and if that meant taking advantage of the other person before he or she could take advantage of you, that was just fine.

She slipped into her spike-heeled shoes and adjusted the belt on her snug knit dress. Again, she surveyed the mirror with smug satisfaction. Even after two kids, Abby still had the figure of a twenty-year-old. Not an *ordinary* twenty-year-old, she thought and smiled, but an extremely *sexy* one. And despite what some of her holier-than-thou neighbors thought—and she knew what people like Karen Fairgate and Laura Avery thought behind those make-believe smiles of theirs—there was nothing wrong with being sexy. Nothing at all.

"Mom!" Olivia Cunningham stuck her head in the doorway and stared impatiently at Abby. "We're going to be late for school again!"

Abby twisted her lip. Ah, the joys of single parenthood!

"Mom, are we gonna be late again?" The high-pitched voice of Brian chimed in from the hallway. "'Cause the teacher said next time I gotta bring a note."

Abby applied one final coat of lip gloss. "Just a sec, you guys. Mommy has to make herself presentable for a job interview this morning." Damn, why did she have to oversleep? She really needed the job at Alcocks. She hoped the job interviewer would be a man. Otherwise, she had picked this dress for nothing. Wait a minute—Abby stopped dead in her tracks. She couldn't get to her interview and drive the kids to school at the same time!

The two children exchanged knowing glances. Olivia tossed her shiny brown hair back over her shoulder and sighed. "Mom, how are me and Brian getting to school today?"

Hastily, Abby reached for her purse and

then gave each child a brief kiss. "I'm really sorry, darlings, but Mommy isn't playing with a full deck this morning." She glanced out the bedroom window and saw Karen Fairgate standing on her lawn dressed in a bathrobe. Honestly, her sister-in-law had no pride. Didn't the woman care how she looked in the morning? Abby Cunningham wouldn't be caught dead outside in a bathrobe like *that!* Wait a minute, there was her answer! She'd get Karen to take the kids to school. Of course, Karen would have to say yes. It wasn't as if she had anything important to do this morning. Karen could be a lady of leisure now that Sid's dealership was doing well.

Abby's thoughts rested for a moment on her older brother. He was a sweet, caring man, but he'd never achieve one tenth of the success he deserved. He would have been a millionaire today if he hadn't insisted on being "Mr. Good Guy." Abby hadn't given up the thought that one day her big brother might ask her for some advice. Abby had some fabulous ideas about making Knots Landing Motors more profitable, if only Sid would listen. On the other hand, Sid's new partner, Gary Ewing, seemed to know what he was doing.

The more Abby saw of her handsome, blond neighbor, the more she was interested. "Intrigued" was a better word. In fact, she'd been thinking quite a lot about

Gary lately. And she wasn't exactly sure why. In any event, he seemed handcuffed to that dewy-eyed ingenue wife of his, Valene. Valene Ewing—Abby gave a deprecating snort. Now, there was *another* woman who didn't know how to dress. Her wardrobe was strictly out of the Lil' Abner comic strip. Valene and Gary Ewing. Abby still hadn't figured that duo out. Married as teenagers. Apart for seventeen years, and then, married again. And Abby thought *her* life was crazy!

''Mom!'' Olivia's young voice registered faint disapproval.

Abby gave her daughter a wink. ''Well, what are you waiting for?'' She strode out into the hallway. ''It's time for school!''

''But, Richard,'' Laura Avery was protesting, ''it's on your way.'' The two of them were standing in their driveway, arguing. ''How often do I ask you to drop Jason at school?''

Richard straightened his tie with irritation. What was his wife's problem, anyhow? What did she want from him now? He had important things to do this morning, and she was going to make him late. It was up to *her* to keep the home front running smoothly. Getting Jason to school was *her* responsibility. It was the second time this month she was asking him to do it. ''Why did you have to spring this on me this morning of all mornings?''

Laura usually obeyed Richard's slightest whim, but today she refused to back down. At a certain point during an argument with Richard her resolve had always weakened, but this time she found a core of iron inside her. She tidied a stray wisp of red hair and brushed an imaginary speck of dust from the collar of her silk blouse. She continued down the driveway, until she reached her car.

"I didn't spring anything on you, Richard," she remarked quietly, realizing he had followed her. "I told you a week ago." She opened the door to the driver's side and climbed inside. "And I reminded you again last night."

Richard refused to let up. He stuck his head through the window. "When did you tell me, Laura? When I was asleep?"

Laura paused. Maybe it was more important for him to be at work on time than it was for her. She felt herself starting to give in again, the way she always gave in. Richard's eyebrow lifted expectantly. And it was then Laura noticed a smug smile twitching at the corner of her husband's mouth. He was waiting, any second, to hear her say she'd changed her mind and would take Jason to school, after all. Something in that smug look irritated Laura. "Richard," she said finally, "I'm sorry. I've got to go now."

His eyes narrowed, as if to silently say, "You'll pay for this one!" But instead, the words coming out of his mouth were "Go ahead, then. Go!" Angrily, he watched her car pull away and disappear around the corner.

"Dad?" Jason Avery tugged at his father's sleeve.

Richard sighed and reached in his suit pocket for his keys. "All right, get in the car, or we're all gonna be late." He started the engine and pulled the car out of the driveway. Unfortunately, it wasn't in time to avoid a very determined Abby Cunningham. Richard was torn between his annoyance at being late for work and absolute admiration of his gorgeous new neighbor. He couldn't believe the sexy outfit she was wearing this morning. Then again, when did Abby Cunningham *not* wear a sexy outfit? She was the kind of woman who made a habit of watering her front lawn dressed in a skimpy bikini. A man could have a million problems on his mind and still notice Abby. The little number she was wearing today molded every curve of her incredible body. And now, she was actually leaning against the driver's window.

"Richard," she purred softly.

Richard preened. "That voice should be outlawed."

Abby Cunningham knew how to approach her target and move in for the kill. "Richard," she pouted in her finest damsel-in-distress fashion, "I'm running a little late for a job interview—''

He nodded understandingly. ''And I'm late for a meeting.''

Abby leaned her supple body closer to Richard. Now, she was close enough for him to smell the exotic fragrance she always wore. He didn't know the name of it, but it was French and very expensive. ''Richard, if I have to drop the kids at school, I'm going to be *so* late.''

Despite the blatant appeal to his masculine ego, Richard didn't deliver the expected response. ''I've got the same problem.''

''Richard,'' she pleaded with her dazzling blue eyes, ''it's only a couple of miles to Anderson.''

''In the wrong direction.'' Richard heard himself answer firmly, but inside he was crumbling. Ever since the woman had moved into the cul-de-sac, Richard couldn't stop thinking about her. He'd even dreamed about her a couple of times. He often found himself wondering what she'd be like in bed. And occasionally, like this very moment, he actually believed that he would soon find out. It was inevitable. On the other hand, maybe it was all in his mind. Maybe Abby was just a big tease. Even if she was divorced and alone. And definitely on the prowl.

''Please. This is *so* important to me.'' Abby enlisted her most sensual tone. ''And anyhow, they'll wait for *you*. You're such a big shot." She paused. "Please?"

The two of them were definitely going to get together one of these days, Richard decided, the blood pounding in his temples. "Sure, I'll take the kids for you."

"Oh, you're such a darling!" Abby gave him a quick peck on the cheek, and gestured triumphantly to Brian and Olivia. "Richard's going to drop you at school!" And with that, Abby Cunningham dashed off to her own car.

Karen Fairgate observed the entire exchange from her front lawn. Once again, Abby had manipulated Richard Avery to do her bidding. Karen was willing to bet a bundle that a potential danger zone was brewing out there. Richard Avery was the kind of man who believed that every woman found him irresistible. What a jerk. She had never cared for him. How could Laura have put up with a self-centered guy like him for so long?

Karen shook her head. If Abby and Richard were having an affair, how long would it take for Abby to lose interest? Probably, not very long at all. That is, if Abby Cunningham and Richard Avery *were* having an affair. Some instinct told Karen that such a point hadn't been reached yet. But Abby was like a cat that enjoyed playing with its prey before pouncing. Then, another instinct told Karen Fairgate to mind her own business.

Chapter Two

And How Was Your Morning?

Of all the times on earth for this to happen—Richard Avery shook his head in disbelief. He was standing in the middle of traffic, gazing down at a flat tire. Damn, why did these things always happen to him? Furiously, he glanced at his watch. This was all Laura's fault, for insisting that he drive Jason to school. Well, he muttered to himself, fumbling in the trunk for the spare tire and a jack, this was the last time he'd allow Laura to have her way. Belatedly, Richard admitted that Abby Cunningham also had a hand in this. If she hadn't sweet-talked him into driving out of his way for her two bratty kids—suddenly, there was the loud screeching of tires and a car horn.

"Hey, you dumb jerk!" bellowed a voice from a passing car. "Keep your damn kids off the road!"

Richard gave a start, and looked up to see his son, Jason, and Brian Cunningham darting perilously close to the traffic. Another oncoming car gave an angry honk, and swerved to avoid the two children.

"Holy mother of—" Richard dropped the lug wrench and lunged for the boys, grabbing one in each arm and pulling them to safety.

"Don't you ever do that again," he chastised them both, his face contorted with fear and anger. "You little idiots almost got yourselves killed!"

"We were just foolin' around, Mr. Avery," Brian protested.

"Yeah, Dad," chimed in Jason.

"Boy, are we ever gonna be late," observed Olivia Cunningham critically.

Richard groaned inwardly and rolled up his shirt-sleeves. By the time he got this tire changed, and the kids dumped off at school, he'd be at least an hour late. Today of all days! He'd planned for weeks what to say at this meeting with L. B. Cargill. This was going to be the morning he made his big move. Well, forget it now. He gave his wristwatch another desperate glance. Damn. Damn! Why did these things always happen to him?

Sid Fairgate pulled the car into his private parking space at Knots Landing Motors and turned off the engine. He didn't get out of the car, though. He just wanted to sit in the driver's seat for another moment and compose himself. For the hundredth time, he went over the events of this morning in his head. He still couldn't understand what had gone wrong. His hands lingered on the blueprints lying on the seat next to him. Before the meeting with the patent attorney, he'd been so sure, so optimistic. The lawyer had been polite, but blunt. The bottom line was this: At the present time, there was nothing he could do for Sid.

So—he gave a sigh, rubbing his hands on the steering wheel—it was back to the drawing board. Disappointment was no stranger to Sid Fairgate. On the other hand, he had learned to be philosophical about the numerous defeats life dished out. There had been, after all, compensations. He had Karen. Sid's heart softened slightly as he thought of his wife. There wasn't another woman like her in the world. And then, there were the kids. Okay, so maybe sometimes they could be wild enough to turn his hair prematurely gray, but on the whole, they were pretty terrific. And bright. When he thought about it, he was luckier than most fathers. Particularly with Eric and Michael. Oddly, in many ways, his sons were his best friends. He found them easier to talk to than most adults.

Sid found himself smiling. Yes, he was

luckier than a lot of people, all things considered. And just because the meeting this morning had been a bust, it didn't mean that he couldn't keep trying. Meanwhile, he still had Knots Landing Motors. All in all, it had been nearly a twenty-five-year struggle to raise the money to buy the dealership and then make it into the success it was today.

Of course, he still wondered if making Gary Ewing his partner had been a wise decision. It wasn't that Gary was hard to get along with, quite the contrary. In fact, Sid Fairgate found both Gary and Valene Ewing two of the most likeable people he'd ever met. And there was no doubting that Gary had a way with potential customers. Even out here in California, the reputation of the Texas oil dynasty was known. And Gary had the undeniable charm his family was famous for. It was just—Sid hesitated—sometimes he wasn't sure what exactly made Ewing tick. And sometimes, a slight nagging doubt warned Sid that Gary might be just a little too fond of shortcuts. Shortcuts in business had never been Sid's way. And he could sense by Gary's increasing restlessness that Knots Landing Motors wasn't turning over the quick profits he desired.

With a sigh, Sid gathered up the blueprints and his briefcase and emerged from the car. As he entered the garage, he saw Gary talking to one of the mechanics. It wasn't until he took a few steps closer that he realized the mechanic was a woman. Despite her grease-stained coveralls, and equally grease-streaked face, he could see the revealing curves of a remarkable figure. Underneath the grime and dirt, he could see the woman was not only young but extremely pretty.

"How'd it go, Sid?" Gary looked up with a smile.

Sid shrugged. It had cost him a hundred and fifty bucks to find out that he was on the right track with his engine, but the attorney had been clear that there was still a long way to go. In any event, he didn't feel like discussing it at the moment. "Sorry about all this. What happened with Orchid Cab?" He continued to stare at the shapely mechanic in puzzlement.

Gary finished signing a work order and handed it to the woman. "It's okay. We pushed back the meeting. They'll be coming in at two-thirty."

"'Morning, Mr. Fairgate," said the woman mechanic, as she turned and walked toward the other end of the garage.

He stared after her. "'Morning." Sid was totally nonplussed. "Who's that?" he asked Gary.

His partner laughed. "Your new mechanic, Linda Striker. Summa cum laude from M.I.T. going for a Ph.D. in advanced automotive design." Gary cast an appreciative glance at her retreating figure. "She's taking a semester off to find out how an engine works—from the inside out."

Uh-huh, thought Sid. But aloud, he said, "I thought we were cutting back." There was just a tinge of rebuke in his voice.

"We're cutting back on salesmen, not repairmen," Gary countered. "The garage is booming. It's what's keeping us afloat." He followed Sid into the showroom.

"I don't know." Sid was unconvinced. "We've never had a lady repairman."

"Repair*person*. If Karen could see your face, she'd report you to the National Organization for Women!"

Sid scratched his head. He just wasn't comfortable with the whole idea. "It looks funny . . . a woman in the shop." There was a thoughtful pause. "I guess I'll get used to it."

Gary flashed a typical Ewing smile. "Hope you do. She's the hardest worker we've got, partner."

As the two men disappeared into the office area, Linda Striker rubbed away some of the grease from her cheek. Gary Ewing, the man who had hired her, was a good-looking, pleasant guy. She had met hundreds like him. The person who impressed her, however, was Sid Fairgate. He wasn't handsome in the classical sense, but there was something undeniably masculine about him. Something *real*. At twenty-two, Linda wasn't interested in the gushing insincerity of younger men. She was ready for a new challenge and a more mature relationship. Someone like Sid Fairgate, maybe. She ran her tongue deliberately over her lower lip. How old could her new boss be? Somewhere in his forties, maybe twice her age, but why did that matter? Of course, with her luck, he probably was married. Still, Linda considered, who knows? She was going to enjoy working at Knots Landing Motors, that was for sure.

The three of them stood in the doorway of the spectacular home, nestled high in the Pacific Palisades. Laura Avery, at her first showing, shyly watched her boss attempt to make a sale.

"Seven-fifty might seem a bit steep if you're used to prices in the East," Scooter was saying, "but believe me, Mrs. Vandenbrooke, you won't find a house in this area for less than a million—not this size on a half acre of land." He paused, waiting to see if she would bite. She didn't. This was one tough customer, Scooter thought. A hard-jawed New Englander who looked older than her real age. Her face brought to mind the society matrons of nineteen-thirties film comedies. The kind of woman one would describe as "handsome." Usually, at this point in a showing, Scooter Warren had the potential client at least interested. Or mildly intrigued, even. But with Mrs. Otis Vandenbrooke, all of the famous Scooter Warren charm was falling flat—the same persuasive salesmanship that had made Warren Realty among the most successful brokers in California. It was quite a blow to his ego, to say the least. Mrs. Otis Vandenbrooke had to be made of stone. Scooter felt a pang of sympathy for *Mr.* Otis Vandenbrooke.

He cleared his throat and gave it another try. "And I'll tell you this. Put in a tennis court—and there's plenty of room for one, believe me—why, you'd be adding another two hundred thousand to the value of your home."

"It's not *my* home yet, Mr. Warren," said Mrs. Vandenbrooke finally, in her most repressive tone.

"*Scooter,*" he insisted.

"Why is everyone in California on a first-name basis?" the client complained.

Scooter cleared his throat. "You've picked a good time to move, Mrs. Vandenbrooke. Why, this is a buyer's market. With interest rates so high, the sellers are in a real squeeze—"

"And so, I imagine, are *you*" was the frigid reproof.

Scooter cast a helpless glance at Laura and decided to give it one last try. "If you and Mr. Vandenbrooke would be willing to come up a little on the cash, I think I might be able to talk them down to seven-ten.''

Mrs. Vandenbrooke gave a disinterested shrug. ''It's not the money, Mr. Warren. It's the house.'' There was a deprecatory pause. ''I'm not so sure about phony Tudor.''

''Well,'' Scooter stammered, ''I wouldn't exactly call it phony—''

Out of the clear blue sky, Laura Avery opened her mouth. It wasn't something she often did at Warren Realty. She was new, and just learning. And all those years of being the obedient housewife to Richard had robbed her of much self-confidence. But suddenly, here she was stepping forward in an impossible situation. She couldn't believe that the words were actually flowing glibly from her.

''Mrs. Vandenbrooke,'' she heard herself remark, with a patina of arrogance, ''every Tudor home built after 1603 is not really authentic. But in this case the architect was Clayton Raphael, a true Anglophile.''

At this point, she noticed that some of the animosity had left the older woman's face. She was actually listening.

''He designed this house for himself,'' she continued, ''basing the entire structure on seventeenth-century plans. Many of the materials were shipped over from England. The beams are authentic, and the flagstone is from Devon.'' She waited, and saw the growing interest in the client's face. ''Of course, if you would prefer something more modern . . .''

''Modern?''

Laura smiled. ''I mean something more authentic.''

Mrs. Vandenbrooke hesitated. ''It *is* rather nicely built,'' she conceded.

Laura nodded confidently. ''Since you're married to an architect, I knew you'd appreciate *that*.''

Scooter watched the entire exchange in fascination. Laura actually had the tough old bird eating out of her hand.

''Do you know my husband's work, Mrs. . . . ?''

''Avery,'' Laura responded. ''Isn't your husband Otis Vandenbrooke? The Copes Tower in Pittsburgh is one of my *favorite* buildings!''

Mrs. Vandenbrooke preened. ''Do you think we might go inside again, Mrs. Avery? I'd like to take another look at the kitchen.''

Laura gave a gracious nod and escorted the woman inside. Scooter might just as well have been invisible. He continued to stare after them with his mouth agape. *Absolutely incredible*, he was thinking. Who ever would have believed that Laura Avery had it in her? After he had given the client up for dead, his quiet little assistant suddenly turned it all around. He never had fully appreciated Laura before, but now he realized that she was a born salesman—

saleswoman. Laura Avery was definitely headed up the career ladder at Warren Realty. She had real potential. He wondered where she had been keeping herself for so long.

Chapter Three

Lunchtime

The imposing logo on the glass doors read PINCUS, SIMPSON AND LYLE, ATTORNEYS-AT-LAW. Richard stared at the raised chrome lettering for a brief instant before he pushed his way through the doors into the lush, carpeted reception area. He was late, fatally late. Richard frantically wiped his sweaty palms against the greasy, smudged summer-weight suit. If it had only been a dark wool instead of this pale shade of blue, he might have been able to get away with it. From the way Millie, the receptionist, was gaping at him, Richard knew he was an unholy mess. Well, he was lucky to have gotten to the office at all. Changing that tire in rush-hour traffic had been an interminable nightmare. Damn!

"Sure you want to go in there like that?" Millie inquired with her distinctive New York twang. There was true concern in her voice, not maliciousness. Millie was one of the few people at the firm who actually liked him.

"Great, just great," Richard muttered.

"Wait a sec." The young woman rummaged in her desk for a minute and handed him a facial tissue.

Gratefully, he accepted it and began to wipe the grime from his face and hands. "Has Cargill gotten here yet?" he asked.

Millie smirked. "Didn't you see the red carpet and brass band?" She gestured toward the main conference room. "In there."

Richard gazed warily in the direction of the closed doors. He felt like a prisoner walking to his own execution. "The conference room," he repeated to himself.

"Hey," Millie suggested with a laugh, "maybe if you bow on the way in, they won't notice the spots."

Richard drew himself up to his full height and with a heavy heart marched to the conference-room door. He took a deep breath, opened the door and walked in. They were all there, in the elegant room with windows overlooking a sweeping panorama of the city. His bosses, the senior partners Pincus and Simpson, were comfortably nestled in the supple leather chairs. And with one elbow propped up against the sleek marble conference table was the man himself, Lynn Baker Cargill, considered one of the finest legal minds in the country. Richard had always dreamed of meeting him, but not like this. A hush fell over the room at Richard's entrance. Simpson, who had been rambling on in his usual long-winded way of kissing up to VIPs, paused and glared at Richard. The glare was full of meaning. It clearly indicated what the senior partner thought of Richard, his appearance, his unpardonable lateness and, more important, his future at the firm. Under Simpson's unrelenting gaze, Richard felt like a drowning man going down for the third time. He made his way to an empty chair.

"Mr. Cargill," Simpson finally said, his tone icy and cutting, "this is Richard Avery, one of the junior associates."

To Richard's amazement, the very important Lynn Baker Cargill rose most imposingly from his seat and extended a gracious hand. "Flat tire, Mr. Avery?" he remarked with some degree of amusement.

The man's eyes were piercing, just as Richard had always heard. Somewhere, he found his voice. "I've been looking forward to meeting you for quite some time, Mr. Cargill." This was the absolute truth, and the other man sensed the sincerity beneath his words. "My last year in Georgetown I wrote an article for the *Law Review* on *Delta Cattle* versus *the State of Illinois*." Richard could feel the heat of Simpson's continuing glare and sensed the narrowing of Mr. Pincus's eyes as he went on. "That was an incredible brief."

Cargill smiled. "It was a long journey from Evanston to the Supreme Court but well worth the trip. I'd like to see that article sometime.

Simpson coughed, annoyed that Richard had stolen away the attention of the esteemed attorney. "As I was saying, Mr. Cargill, most of the environmental groups protesting the pipeline are small, disorganized, underfunded and, unless they manage to attract the attention of the press—"

"They *have* attracted the attention of the press!" interrupted Cargill, unceremoniously dumping the contents of his briefcase out onto the marble table. "Why the hell else do you think I'm here?" He tossed newspaper clippings to all ends of the marble slab. "If we were just dealing with environmental groups like the Abalone Army and Friends of the Sea Otters, I wouldn't need the services of your law firm. I could take those piddling groups on by myself and never leave Chicago. But we're talking about the California Coastal Commission—not some bunch of daisy-throwing crackpots." He shoved his hands into the pockets of his expensive Italian slacks. "That commission has money, political clout and enough influence to make this easement look like another Three Mile Island." His eyes bored holes into the senior partners. "Let's not kid ourselves, gentlemen. Arkansas Gas and Fuel has got a problem—a three-hundred-million-dollar problem that they're paying *us* to solve." Cargill looked at his watch. "I've got a one o'clock lunch with Charlie Flagg, and I'd sure like to tell our client he's going to get his pipeline."

Richard watched silently as Mr. Pincus turned apoplectic. "I thought you'd moved for a postponement of the prelim," he protested.

Cargill shook his head impatiently. He was beginning to think Pincus and Simpson, despite their prestigious reputation, were a couple of lightweights. "The motion was denied. The hearing will take place as originally scheduled."

Another ghastly silence in the room. "I'm sorry to hear that, sir," Pincus replied hastily. "We were under the impression that this would be merely an exploratory meeting."

Lynn Baker Cargill rose from the table to his full height, in the same imperious manner that he had often used before juries. "I don't have time for exploratory meetings. I suggest we table this till after lunch." His dissatisfaction with the law firm of Pincus, Simpson and Lyle was evident in every cutting word. "Maybe by then you fellas will have rolled up your sleeves, put on your thinking caps and come up with something for tomorrow."

If Laura Avery had been able to see what

her husband did next, she might have laughed at the striking similarities to her own experience of the morning. Just as Laura had unexpectedly retrieved the situation for Warren Realty, Richard suddenly stood up and did the same thing for Pincus, Simpson and Lyle. "Excuse me, Mr. Cargill—" he found his own voice again, and it was unusually smooth and confident "—but there was a case a few weeks ago in northern California—"

"What case was that, Mr. Avery?" interrupted Mr. Pincus tightly. As far as the senior partner was concerned, Richard was an upstart who didn't know his place.

From nowhere, Richard drew out a clipping. He had eyes only for the prestigious lawyer from Chicago. *The hell with Pincus,* he thought. This was his big chance. "It didn't receive much attention in the Los Angeles press, so some people might have missed it. It concerns the Diamond Pulp and Paper Company, and how they won an easement to run a chemical pipeline through the Dubakella National Forest."

"I hardly think—" Pincus began pompously.

"Excuse me," interjected Cargill, "but could I see that article?"

Smiling inwardly, Richard handed him the clipping and waited as the other attorney examined it.

Cargill finally looked up, a pleased

expression on his face. "Mr. Avery, are you free for lunch? I like a man who does his homework."

I'm on my way, Richard shouted to himself, as he followed Cargill out of the conference room. Pincus and Simpson were two incompetent hacks, as far as he was concerned.

"How do you feel about boats, Mr. Avery?" Cargill inquired as they walked toward the immense double glass doors.

"I think they're terrific," Richard replied, winking at a stunned Millie as he passed the reception desk. Maybe this was going to turn out to be *his* day, after all.

Linda Striker didn't know what hit her. One moment, she was working quickly and efficiently loosening the lug nuts of a flat tire; the next moment, as she pulled the third lug nut loose, the entire car came toppling down off the rear jack. With a horrifying crash, the back end of the car smashed to the concrete floor. Linda rolled away just in time to avoid being crushed.

"What the hell?" cried out Sid, who had been working nearby on another car. He rushed over, his face a combination of anger and concern. "You all right?" He helped Linda up from the floor. "Where did you get this jack?" he examined the device with annoyance. "From the trunk?"

Linda was flushed with embarrassment. "I would have put it up on the hydraulic, but they're all being used," she tried to explain. Inside, she was quaking. Sid Fairgate looked furious. "I'm sorry," Linda offered. "I promised Mrs. McGuane I'd have the car ready by noon. I'm sorry," she repeated. This was it, she thought. She'd really blown the job.

Sid was down on his knees examining the damage to the car. He exhaled heavily. "Looks like it bent the axle." There was a pause, and he stared at Linda. "You're lucky. You might have lost a hand or a foot."

"I'll . . . I'll pay for the damage." Linda Striker was close to tears, but she struggled to sound calm.

Sid shook his head in disbelief. "Didn't you put on the hand brake?"

Well, she *thought* she had. She was stupid, that's all. Today of all days. Her first day on the job. Linda had changed hundreds of tires before. Of all the rotten luck. But worst of all, she looked incompetent in front of Sid Fairgate, a man she had wanted to impress ever since meeting him this morning. She couldn't stand to see the disapproval on his rugged face. "Mr. Fairgate, maybe I don't know my way around an engine the way you do, but this was an honest mistake."

"I can't afford honest mistakes," Sid finally said. "I'm running a garage here, not a graduate school."

Karen entered the service bay just at this

awkward moment. She noticed the tall, attractive woman in overalls, eyes slightly downcast. A *very* attractive young woman in overalls. What was going on here? "Now I see why you don't come home for lunch," she said as she walked up behind Sid. "How do you do?" She extended her hand to Linda. "I'm Karen Fairgate."

To the pretty mechanic, who was still waiting to hear if she was going to lose her new job, this was yet another blow. Sid Fairgate was married. Her heart sank as she shook Karen's hand. "Linda Striker," she introduced herself. "Nice to meet you, Mrs. Fairgate." *Mrs. Fairgate*—it was almost painful to say the words. Darn, did the woman have to be so good-looking and bubbly? The confident, outgoing creature standing before her made Linda feel positively gawky.

Karen's attention went back to Sid, who seemed intent on making a decision. Karen wondered what this was all about. "So, what happened with the lawyer?" she asked casually, not wanting to appear ruffled. Instinctively, however, Karen's radar was up.

Sid took Karen's arm affectionately. "I'll tell you at lunch," he explained, leading her away. Then, he paused and turned back to Linda. "Call Sheila McGuane and tell her what happened. Maybe Gary can arrange for a loaner."

The significance of his words was not

lost on the young mechanic. She still had the job!

As Karen walked to the car with Sid, she couldn't help saying softly, "A lady mechanic at Knots Landing Motors? My, my! We *are* making progress!"

Sid appeared embarrassed. "Gary hired her."

Karen grinned. "Uh-huh. She looks . . . intelligent."

"Brilliant," Sid agreed, so quickly that Karen felt momentarily uncomfortable until her husband continued, "Summa cum laude from M.I.T. and she can't change a tire."

The news pleased Karen more than she could express, but she wasn't sure why. In all her years of marriage, she had never felt threatened by another woman. Now Karen was wondering why, in the space of five minutes, she suddenly felt vulnerable.

"I'm in the mood for a cheeseburger with plenty of onions and fries," Sid was saying.

Karen, whose mouth had been watering all morning for exactly the same repast, now pictured Linda Striker and her slim young figure. Her appetite flew out the window. "And here my heart was set on a fruit salad."

Laura pored over her textbook, preparing for her real estate licensing exam. She munched on a deli salad as she tested herself with possible questions. "Patent," she drilled. "Conveyance of title to government land." So far so good, she thought. "Laches." Okay—she continued, "Delay or negligence in asserting one's legal rights."

Scooter stood unnoticed in the doorway for a moment. He watched her with amusement and then parroted, "'The flagstone's from Devon.' 'Seventeenth-century plans.'" He grinned, then added, "'The Copes Tower is one of my *favorite* buildings!'" He walked into the room. "Boy! Why bother to take the exam?"

Laura was mortified. "I guess I should have kept my mouth shut, huh?"

Scooter looked at her as if she were from another planet. "Kept your mouth shut, are you *kidding?*" He was grinning from ear to ear as he sat down on the edge of Laura's desk. "Mrs. Vandenbrooke wants the house."

"I don't believe it." Laura practically choked on her salad.

"Would I lie?" Scooter asked expansively. "Just got off the phone. You and your big mouth just made us a seven-hundred-and-fifty-thousand-dollar sale!" He leaned across the desk and gave her a big kiss.

Laura sat there, stunned. "You aren't kidding?"

Scooter shook his head, picked up Laura's container of salad and deftly pitched it into the wastebasket. "You can say goodbye to this. No rabbit food for my whiz kid. I'm buying you lunch." He stood up and walked around the desk, reaching for Laura's hand. "Let's go. Vandenbrooke's coming here at three to fill out the loan agreement."

Laura was elated, but then she remembered. "Oh, Scooter, I can't. I've got to pick up Jason at school later this afternoon."

Scooter tossed this off. "Tell him to take a cab." He put a hand on Laura's shoulder. "Seriously, Mrs. V. asked for you *specifically*. It's essential that you be here. Can't you call Richard or one of the neighbors?"

Laura hesitated. "Richard will kill me if I bother him at work."

For some reason, this annoyed Scooter greatly. He didn't know Laura's husband very well, but he didn't like him at all. He impressed Scooter as the kind of man who insisted that his own life come first. Scooter felt that Richard didn't fully appreciate what he had in Laura. He couldn't imagine how Richard Avery managed to instill such unerring devotion in his wife. If his own wife had been as loyal, he would have been a happier man today. Scooter stopped himself. He wasn't going to think of that now. "Look, Laura," he said firmly. "What about *your* work? This isn't a hobby, it's your career. C'mon. Call him. You can blame it on me."

"I suppose I could leave the number of the restaurant." Laura was still overwhelmed with guilt. Why did she always feel so guilty about asking Richard to help her out?

Scooter took advantage of her hesitation. "Sure, and if there's a problem, he can call you there. Okay?"

Laura sighed. "Okay," she conceded at last.

Scooter grinned from ear to ear. "Great. I almost thought I'd have to kidnap you. Are you as hungry as I am?"

Laura smiled weakly. As much as she'd enjoy lunch with the boss, Richard was going to be furious with her. He didn't like being inconvenienced.

"I could eat just about anything," Scooter chattered brightly. "What do you think about *nouvelle* cuisine?" He hesitated. "On the other hand, do you like Thai food? There's a terrific place over on the Pacific Coast Highway."

Laura followed her boss out of the office. This was an important day for her. Her first major sale, and she wasn't even licensed yet. She was so proud she wanted to shout it from the rooftops. She was on her way at last.

Chapter Four

Win Friends and Influence People

The impressive, sea-going yacht at anchor in the marina bore the unprepossessing name S.S. *Charlie's Rubber Ducky*. Richard had just finished a sumptuous luncheon of sole Véronique and tiger prawns in the company of L. B. Cargill, Charlie Flagg and Flagg's blond secretary, Miss Vesper. He watched the undulating motion of the spectacular body beneath her thin silk dress as she leaned over to light Flagg's cigar.

Richard could hardly believe his good fortune. The events of the past few hours were like some incredible dream. Here he was, sitting on the afterdeck of Charles Flagg's yacht. Charles Flagg, one of the richest men in America. And on the other side of him sat Lynn Baker Cargill, one of the most prestigious lawyers in the country. The mealtime conversation was exactly the type Richard had imagined took place in the salons of the rich and powerful. By the time Flagg's impeccable manservant passed out the cigars and brandy, Richard was in seventh heaven. It was all like being in some glamorous movie, with the warm midday sun glittering down on the water. He was determined to savor every moment of this, and he found the taste of wealth and success intoxicating. This cigar, for example, was a pre-Castro Havana. Richard inhaled the mellow aroma appreciatively and listened to the ongoing exchange between the two powerhouses. It never failed to fascinate him how business lunches followed the subtle trajectory from small talk to hard sell. It was here that the conversation grew serious. Charlie Flagg was a man who was used to having his own way, and he proceeded to curse the main obstacle to his desired pipeline.

"Damn Coastal Commission," the skipper of the S.S. *Rubber Ducky* boomed. "One lousy sixteen-inch pipe, and you'd think I was planning to build a nuclear reactor across the street from Grauman's Chinese Theater." He waved his cigar in the air, scattering the ashes. "Preliminary hearing! I want to end it tomorrow, you understand?"

"Loud and clear, Charlie," Cargill agreed.

"For cryin' out loud," Flagg continued, "these jokers are costing me a million each day this goes on. So, what exactly do you plan on telling 'em?"

The other man took a long drag of his cigar. "For one thing, I'm going to mention the Diamond Pulp and Paper Company. It's a precedent that Mr. Avery is familiar with."

"Sounds promising," said Miss Vesper, speaking up for the first time. She had a voice like velvet.

"I'll want the results of the stress tests on the pipe, Miss Vesper." Cargill smiled at her vaguely.

"We've got that information," the stunning secretary replied.

Cargill put his hands up in the air. "I'm sorry about the postponement, Charlie. It's not going to be easy, but I know we can dig up a few more goodies before tomorrow morning." He paused significantly. "What do you think, Richard?"

Richard preened slightly. "This is an excellent cigar," he replied. He was delighted to hear Charles Flagg laugh uproariously at his response. The others joined in, and Richard felt a warm inner glow growing inside him.

A while later, Richard and Cargill leaned against the railing of the yacht, enjoying the sight of a bikini-clad Miss Vesper. She was engaged in rubbing suntan lotion on the bare back of her employer. Charlie Flagg sat on his chaise longue in swimming trunks. He was talking loudly and animatedly on the phone. Richard couldn't hear everything Flagg was shouting into the receiver but the conversation was tantalizing, sprinkled with tidbits such as "Sell! Sell!" and "Middle East" and "Libya."

Cargill finished his cigar and gazed out over the railing. "You handle yourself very well, Richard. I must admit I'm impressed."

Richard finished his own cigar. "I wish you'd mention that to Mr. Simpson. After nine years, I'm still pushing papers in the only office without a window."

Cargill smiled cryptically. "Maybe you're with the wrong firm."

Richard decided to test the water. "I'm thirty-seven. I can't start from the bottom again. Whenever I shop around, I'm competing with hotshots fresh from law school."

"If we weren't staring into the Pacific Ocean, I'd say 'Go west, young man.'"

Richard paused. "How about east?"

Cargill raised an eyebrow. "As far east as Chicago?"

Now Richard decided to go for it. The water was warm. Now was the time to take the plunge. "You're the kind of lawyer I'd like to be, Mr. Cargill. If you want me in Chicago, that's where I'll go."

Cargill gave a vague nod and chose his next words carefully. "If we win this case, you might find you're pointing in the right direction." He paused. "If we win, Richard."

The full significance of Cargill's answer finally sank in. Richard realized that this was a promise only as good as the results the older lawyer required. Everything in Richard's future depended on the hearing tomorrow. Whatever it took, he decided, whatever was required, Richard would do. Even if he had to stay up all night in the law library. The rewards would be well worth the effort. In his mind he pictured his glorious departure from Pincus, Simpson and Lyle. He would leave Knots Landing behind in the dust for a phenomenal new beginning in Chicago and the prestigious law practice of L. B. Cargill. And one day—Richard practically licked his lips in anticipation—he would be a partner. "Cargill and Avery," he liked the ring of that. Better yet, "Avery and Cargill." Richard chuckled and tossed his cigar over the railing into the silver waves lapping alongside the yacht.

It had been a phenomenal day for Laura Avery. Scooter had succeeded in convincing her that a celebration lunch was in order. He had whisked her off to an elegant bistro in the most fashionable district of Knots Landing. Laura had never set foot inside Chez François before. Karen Fairgate had once joked to her that most people had to apply for a bank loan to afford an appetizer at the ultra-exclusive restaurant. But when Laura arrived at Chez François with Scooter, they were greeted effusively by François himself and personally escorted to a prime table.

"I come here quite a bit," Scooter admitted, slightly embarrassed.

As they sipped Chablis from fine lead crystal, Laura noticed for the first time that her boss looked almost boyish. Odd, she had never realized before how utterly likable he was—from the eager way he insisted they share several exotic appetizers down to the genuine pleasure Scooter took in ordering the most sinful French pastries for dessert.

"What do you *mean* you don't have any room left for a Napoleon?" he declared in mock outrage. "Do you think this is some *ordinary* run-of-the-mill Napoleon?" He paused dramatically and pointed to the other dessert plate. "And what about this fresh fruit tart? Do you realize how many raspberries gave their lives for this tart, Laura? Well, *do* you?" He put a napkin over his eyes. "Have some compassion, Avery."

Perhaps it was the wine, but in another second Laura was bubbling over with laughter. It felt good to be in the company of Scooter. He was such a nice man, and so easygoing. It was somewhat of a contradiction, because Scooter Warren had a well-deserved reputation as a hard-hitting businessman. Yet, strangely, he lacked a kind of intensity that had always made Laura uncomfortable. She confessed to herself that it was a quality in Richard she had never cared for. Still, she loved Richard. Of course she loved Richard. No matter what his flaws, he was still her life.

"All right, if you insist—I'll split the Napoleon with you, Avery." Scooter's ebullient voice shattered her reverie. There was always an edge of laughter in everything Scooter Warren said, but that wasn't the only pleasant aspect of being in his company. He was lavish yet at the same time sincere with his compliments. Right now, Laura was eating it all up. She needed all the compliments she could get. At home, they were few and far between.

She looked at her watch and realized how quickly the time had passed. "It's almost ten of three!" she exclaimed.

"The lovely Mrs. Vandenbrooke awaits," Scooter said and grinned, taking one last regretful mouthful of raspberry tart.

Laura nodded. "Even from here, Mr. Warren, I can hear your heart pounding with eager anticipation."

"Yes, I confess," Scooter said with a playful sigh, "it was love at first sight. I assume you saw the sparks fly between us."

"Indeed," Laura agreed solemnly. "But your secret is safe with me, boss."

"I knew I could rely on your discretion," Scooter answered lightly, as he motioned for the check. There was a pause. "All kidding aside, Laura, you really impressed the hell out of me today. I don't often see someone of your caliber in the business. It won't be long before you can write your own ticket."

Laura flushed with pride at the compliment. "I just want to be good at my job."

Scooter signed the bill. "You're going to be outstanding." He grasped her hand briefly. "And I'm going to be damn proud of you, Laura Avery."

Ten minutes later, they were back inside Scooter's office. Mrs. Vandenbrooke was ensconced in Scooter's highbacked leather chair and was signing the loan forms.

"It's a fabulous house, Mrs. Vandenbrooke, and an incredible price. You know, I almost bought it myself."

Mrs. Vandenbrooke didn't look up from the pile of papers. "What stopped you?"

Scooter shrugged helplessly. "My wife's a Williamsburg Colonial freak."

"How unfortunate for you." The older woman sniffed. "Goodness," she declared as Scooter continued to hand her more forms. "I haven't signed my name so many times since my first husband flew his Cherokee Banshee into Mount Whitney and left no will . . . the fool."

Laura valiantly suppressed a cough and attempted to look solemn. She had never met anyone like Mrs. Otis Vandenbrooke.

"Here's the last of them." Scooter handed another loan form across the desk.

"Thank heaven." Mrs. Vandenbrooke inspected the heavily bejeweled fingers of her right hand. "I've got writer's cramp."

"How long an escrow do you think you'll need?" Scooter inquired, handing the sheaf of papers to Laura.

Mrs. Vandenbrooke gave an indifferent shrug. "Thirty days should be sufficient."

Laura tried to conceal her surprise. "Are you sure you don't want more time?"

"How long does it take to pack?" was the sardonic reply.

Laura wondered what kind of brightly wrapped package was this wealthy client's life. One thing was sure—Mrs. Vandenbrooke was the least sentimental woman Laura had ever met. She hesitated—that was, with the exception of Abby Cunningham. Just conjuring up the image of her nubile neighbor made Laura distinctly uncomfortable. She'd tried not to notice the way Abby looked at Richard when she thought Laura wasn't watching. Of course, Abby Cunningham gave that "come hither" look of hers to every man in Knots Landing, so initially it hadn't bothered Laura too much. The disturbing part was that, lately, Richard was looking back. That was all right, though. Laura supposed she could live with it, as long as Richard just "looked." Besides, though perhaps it was wishful thinking, recently Laura had gotten the impression that Abby Cunningham had her gun sights set on bigger game. She perceived that indirectly it had to do with Abby's precarious financial status.

Everyone in the cul-de-sac knew that Abby was struggling to find a job. Normally, Laura's heart went out to any single mother. Besides, those kids of hers, Brian and Olivia, were almost as lovable as her own Jason. Laura smiled tightly. Why worry about Abby? That blond bombshell wouldn't be struggling for very long. If anyone was capable of mixing pleasure with business, it was definitely Abby Cunningham.

Scooter had risen from his seat to shake Mrs. Vandenbrooke's hand ceremoniously. "How about a drink? I think we all have something to celebrate."

Mrs. Vandenbrooke replaced her solid gold pen inside her suede clutch. "I'll celebrate when I've moved in, thank you, but I certainly could do with a drink." She looked at Laura, and for the first time all day, the corners of her mouth actually began to twitch upward in a hint of a genuine smile. "And you, Mrs. Avery?"

Laura sighed regretfully. She enjoyed feeling like part of the team. It might have been fun to join in the festivities, but there were Richard and Jason to consider. It was getting on toward dinnertime. "I'd love to, but my husband and son are waiting at home." She paused. "I have to make dinner for them." As soon as the words were out of her mouth she realized how ludicrous they sounded, almost as if she were Cinderella and her coach was about to turn into a pumpkin.

Mrs. Vandenbrooke apparently read Laura's mind. There was a shade of sympathy in her tone as she walked over and patted Laura's hand. "The strange thing is, they never say thank you, do they, Mrs. Avery?"

In that split second, Laura decided she liked Mrs. Otis Vandenbrooke. Maybe she wasn't as cold as she appeared to be.

"I beg your pardon, Mrs. Vandenbrooke?" Scooter interjected. He felt like he was being excluded from a private joke.

"You had to be there, Mr. Warren" was the client's level reply, as she continued to stare knowingly at Laura. Her voice softened. "Let's make it *two* drinks. We don't want them to take you for granted."

Laura considered. Wonderful, exhilarating days like this didn't come along very often. And it had been such a lovely one. Soon it would be over, so why not make it last just a little longer? She brushed back a wisp of red hair from her forehead. "By all means, Mrs. Vandenbrooke. Let's have that drink."

Scooter gave her a delighted wink as he followed the two of them out of the office.

* * *

Sid Fairgate felt uncomfortable and was wondering why. Maybe it had been the long day, or maybe he was suffering from an overactive imagination, but something about the two men sitting in the showroom next to Gary bothered him in the gut. Oh, on the surface Frank Korshak and Roy Lance appeared to be two ordinary businessmen. As the West Coast representatives of Orchid Cab and Delivery, they spoke glibly yet were able to back up their words with facts and figures.

The Roy character looked like a male model in a magazine shirt ad. The three-piece suit he wore had all the markings of an exclusive Bond Street tailor. And he talked like a Harvard M.B.A. Well, not exactly. If Sid hadn't felt a nagging discomfort, he might have laughed. Roy Lance spoke like a combination of a Harvard M.B.A. and the storyteller from *Arabian Nights*. With impressive data, he proceeded to weave a fantastic tale of lightning growth and profit in small passenger transportation. And Gary Ewing was listening with the rapt fascination of a young sultan; he didn't know when to hold back or how to mask his feelings. With every word Roy Lance spoke, Gary's eyes lit up, making it clear he wished to be included in any Orchid Cab business scheme.

Sid shifted restlessly in his seat. Didn't Ewing know that, in business conferences, a person was never supposed to reveal his hand? Or show any emotion? Gary looked ready to plunge into the deal without finding out how deep the water was at his end of the swimming pool. Sid had struggled for twenty-five years to make his dream of a successful dealership come true. He had achieved his goal by hard work and patience. Maybe he was a bit too conservative in some of his business practices, but the fast buck always made him suspicious. He hoped Gary Ewing wasn't going to try to rush him into anything.

Something about Frank Korshak was beginning to make Sid very uneasy. He couldn't quite put his finger on it. Underneath his expensive cashmere coat, Korshak gave off an aura of menace. He was heavyset and unsmiling and had a voice like poured cement. But perhaps it was Sid's imagination. Maybe he shouldn't rush to judgment. The truth was, he didn't want to be in the office right now discussing limousine fleet deals. He was restless and aching to get back to the garage and work on his engine. Right now, wouldn't it be great to put on his overalls, munch on a handful of walnuts and work some more kinks out of the engine?

"By combining the efficiency of a large-scale fleet operation with the personalized service of driver-owned vehicles, we reduce overhead." Roy Lance looked up from his portfolio. "In this way, it pro-

vides a flexible base for expansion depend-
ing on the needs of the community. In this
case, we believe the growing need for our
services."

Frank Korshak stubbed out his cigarette
in the ashtray. "We're talking cabs here.
Plenty of cabs." He looked at Sid expectantly.

"I see." Sid felt a response was required
of him.

"Denver. Phoenix. Albuquerque." Korshak leaned back in his chair. "We're getting pretty big."

Sid nodded. "Sounds impressive, but
Knots Landing is a small town." It was
time to get to the point. "How many cars
do you think you'll need?"

Lance brushed an imaginary piece of lint
from his suit. "We've selected Knots Landing for a pilot program in the Los Angeles
area. We'll begin on a modest scale, of
course," Lance replied. "Say, fifteen vehicles."

Gary's eyes lit up like a little kid's at
Christmastime. "Fifteen?"

Korshak smiled expansively. "For
starters. . . ."

Gary Ewing looked at Sid. He could
hardly believe their good fortune. Sid
remarked calmly, "If you really want fifteen cars, I'll knock six percent off the
sticker price." Sid waited for Korshak's
response, knowing there would be a hook.
It all sounded too good to be true, and Sid

Fairgate did not believe in fairytales.

Korshak ran his tongue over his lower lip with mannered thoughtfulness. "Clark Coollidge offered eleven."

Gary jumped in immediately. "I think we could live with eight and a half—plus a three-year warranty, parts and labor."

Sid shot Gary a sharp glance. "We'll have to talk about that." The four men lapsed into silence.

Frank Korshak slowly rose to his feet, making it clear that the meeting had come to a close. There was nothing left to say. He was a man of few words, and he had already said them all. He made no further attempts to be gracious. A curt nod was the most effusive goodbye Frank Korshak could manage.

Quickly, Roy Lance rose to his feet, gathering up all his papers. He extended his hand in his best prep school manner and said to Sid, "Can I give you a call in the morning?"

Sid shook hands. "I'm here at nine," he replied simply. With amusement, he noticed that Frank Korshak was already halfway out the door.

Gary hopped up from his seat and extended his own hand to Roy Lance. "I'm sure we can do business," he said eagerly. "Just give us a chance to iron out the details."

Lance shook Gary's hand perfunctorily. "Pleasure." He nodded a final time to Sid and then followed his boss out the door.

When the two men had finally disappeared into the parking lot, Gary rubbed
his hands together gleefully. "Fifteen
cars!"

Sid didn't respond. He was watching
Lance and Korshak get into their sleek
black automobile. If the two of them drove
away and never came back, that was all
right with him. Frankly, he'd been relieved
when Korshak had refused his initial offer.
He was secretly hoping the potential deal
would fall through so he wouldn't have to
do business with Orchid Cab. Something
about it smelled like a dead fish.

"Fifteen cars," Gary exclaimed again.
"Can you believe it?"

"No, I can't," Sid replied firmly. "If you
really want to know, I can't believe it at
all." Through all his years in the business,
he'd seen people like Korshak and Lance
come and go. The one thing they all
seemed to have in common was they
always wanted something for nothing.
He'd have to talk to Gary about restraining
his eagerness to make quick deals. Actually, he felt a twinge of sympathy for his
new partner. Gary was really trying to
make something of himself. It hadn't been
easy for the guy, coming from such a pow-
erhouse family. And Gary had an impressive sales ability. Customers loved him.
Instinctively, people trusted him, or at
least, wanted to trust him.

Occasionally Sid felt something like envy of his partner. Sid Fairgate was not the kind of man who often envied other men. But about Gary Ewing, Sid was truly bewildered. Apparently, the man had been born with everything. Family. Wealth. Prestige. Why did a person throw away a deal like that? Sid's own childhood had been one never-ending struggle, and love had been in rather short supply. He'd have given anything to be a member of a thriving extended family like the legendary Ewings. Besides, nature had been abnormally kind to Gary Ewing. Not only had he been given all the material comforts and benefits of family ties, but he had the unbelievable fortune to look like a blond Viking.

Sid Fairgate suppressed a chuckle. He'd always wanted to look like a blond Viking. Not that Sid was vain—it was just every now and then, when he stood in front of the bathroom mirror, his face covered with lather, that he'd start to wonder. What would happen if, when he'd shaved all the foam away, he looked like another person? What if he didn't look so *ordinary*? The only person who thought his face wasn't ordinary was Karen. She once said that when she first laid eyes on him all those years ago, she thought he was the cutest guy she'd ever seen. Well, perhaps love did that. And, whether or not he looked at Karen through the eyes of love, Sid still thought she was beautiful. From the moment they met, Karen had knocked him down for the count.

"Sid," Gary said impatiently, "I really think we should consider Lance's offer."

"It's not much of an offer," Sid remarked dryly.

"Are you kidding?" Gary replied. "They want a fleet deal, for heaven's sake. It's our chance to move fifteen cars. Fifteen gas hogs. Those tanks are starting to gather dust on the lot." Gary thrust his hands in his trouser pockets. "Getting 'em off our hands would be a blessing."

"Really?" Sid indifferently fidgeted with a paper clip on the desk.

"Sure, they'd be doing us a favor."

"A favor, huh?" Sid wanted to laugh.

"I really was impressed by Roy Lance," Gary remarked, folding his arms across the front of his chest. "That guy has got class *and* brains."

Sid groaned to himself. But aloud he answered, "You're quite right. He certainly does have brains."

"I mean, the man really knows what he's talking about," Gary continued.

"Maybe someone should award him the Nobel Prize," Sid shot back.

Gary scratched his head, a truly baffled expression flooding his face. "Sid, correct me if I'm wrong . . . but why do I get the impression you don't take them seriously?"

Sid folded his hands behind his head and stretched back in his chair. "If you get that impression, it's because you're quite right. I don't take Roy Lance *or* Frank Korshak seriously." Sid stood up. "You shouldn't either."

Gary watched him quietly. Sometimes, he couldn't figure Sid Fairgate out. Didn't he understand how badly Knots Landing Motors needed a sale this big? A major infusion of capital like this could work wonders. When would they have another opportunity to unload all those cars? Cars that, Gary had always thought personally, were just white, gas-guzzling elephants. It was cars like those that made Ewing Oil the power it was today. If more people drove those full-size automotive dinosaurs, the price of oil would probably go up ten dollars a barrel, simply as an illustration of the law of supply and demand.

"Honestly, Sid," Gary cajoled, "can we really afford to let an opportunity like this one pass us by?"

Sid sighed. "I'll tell you what. Let me check a few things out first, okay?"

"Such as?"

"I'd like to know a little more about Orchid Cab and Delivery before I make a decision one way or the other."

"What else do you need to know?" Gary couldn't understand Sid's reticence. He hated moving slowly. Sometimes, Sid plodded along like a turtle.

"Don't give me a hard time about this," Sid said firmly. "I know what I'm doing."

Gary gave a nod of silent acquiescence, but on the inside, he remained unconvinced. Perhaps this was one deal that he should work on alone.

Chapter Five

Rumblings of Discontent

When Richard Avery arrived home early that evening, it was to make the annoying discovery that his wife, Laura, was nowhere in sight. Dinner was not cooking in the kitchen, as expected. No perfectly mixed cocktail was waiting to be served to him.

"So, where's Mom?" Jason threw his schoolbooks down on the couch.

"Working," Richard replied tersely. It was bad enough receiving the eleventh-hour message to pick up their son at school. But not to be greeted after a long day was adding insult to injury. What had gotten into Laura lately? Why was she making life so difficult all of a sudden? She insisted on making that worthless little job at Warren Realty such a priority. As if it were ever going to amount to something more than a dinky nine-to-five position. *He* was the one bringing the real money home. Well, he decided firmly, when Laura finally came home, he'd have it out with her. He'd let her know where he stood on this. It was very admirable that she wanted to ''better'' herself. But she had to know where to draw the line.

''Dad, I'm hungry!'' Jason whined.

''Join the club,'' muttered Richard, tossing his briefcase onto the carpet with increasing irritation.

''What are we gonna eat?'' his son asked, persisting.

''That's what we'll find out.'' Richard rolled his eyes and walked into the kitchen. He started rummaging through the refrigerator and the freezer compartment. Damn, there was nothing already prepared. Just some wilted lettuce, a lot of bread and several gallons of gourmet ice cream.

''Ice cream's fine with me, Dad,'' Jason announced positively.

''I'm quite sure it would be,'' Richard retorted. He thrust open the wood-paneled kitchen cabinets and perused the shelves. Chicken noodle soup. Chunk light tuna. Wheat crackers. He suppressed a grumble. This was quite a selection—a real comedown from sole Véronique and truffles. Once more, he savored the memory of the lunch on Flagg's yacht. It was aggravating not to be able to tell Laura about his triumph. One thing he had to hand to his wife was that she normally was an excellent listener. She'd be waiting for him when he came home, ready to hear all about his day. She'd massage the back of his neck where it ached from the strain of all the garbage that they usually dished out to him at Simpson, Pincus and Lyle. Well, Richard decided, they wouldn't be dishing it out much longer if everything went according to plan. Even if it took him all night, he'd find the information necessary to help Lynn Baker Cargill win that easement.

But at the moment, there were more mundane matters to consider. What were he and his starving son going to eat? He flung open the freezer compartment door again and examined the neatly stacked packages. Frozen hamburger patties. Frozen chicken breasts. Frozen leg of lamb. There was a major disadvantage in having a wife who was a gourmet cook. She insisted on preparing everything from scratch. He wished Laura had lapsed from her high culinary standards just long enough to lay in a supply of TV dinners.

Well, he had to select something. Richard eyed the neat stack of wax-papered hamburger patties. The very thought of a burger made him nauseated— it was the one food he had despised since his law school days, when it had been his primary sustenance. He decided on the small leg of New Zealand spring lamb.

How hard could it be to just toss it in the microwave?

"Oh, yuck!" Jason commented. "I'd rather have ice cream."

Richard ignored the boy's comment and began to unwrap the joint of meat. He wondered how long it would take to defrost. The thing was like a chunk of granite.

"I bet Mom is on her way home right now," Jason offered hopefully. The prospect of his dad cooking dinner was not Jason's idea of fun.

Richard took another look at the challenging hunk of rock-solid meat and reached for the wall phone. He dialed the office number of Warren Realty. Once again, it was a battle of wits with the receptionist.

"Mrs. Avery has gone for the day." the woman on the other end of the line said.

"You told me she was out to lunch."

"She came back from lunch. Now she's gone for the day."

Richard was exasperated. "What do you mean she's gone for the day? When did she leave?"

"About an hour ago." There was a pause. "Oh, she's probably at the restaurant."

Richard groaned inwardly. "How can she be at the restaurant if she already came back from lunch? Besides, I already called Chez François and they told me she left hours ago,'' he grumbled.

"That was lunch. Didn't I just say she came back from lunch?''

What was this? Richard wondered.

"Mrs. Avery went to *dinner*,'' the receptionist continued.

"What?'' Richard was stunned. That was great, just great. So nice of his wife to let him know.

"Yes, she went with Mr. Warren and a client.''

"Do me a favor,'' Richard said acidly. "Tell her, if she bothers to check in, that her husband called. He's standing in the kitchen with a hungry child—'' he brought his fist down on the leg of lamb ''—and a block of ice in his hand.''

"I beg your pardon, Mr. Avery?'' the baffled receptionist inquired.

"Never mind. I'm on an ice diet.'' Richard hung up the receiver so forcefully that it bounced off the wall and onto the counter, dangling over the edge on its short, spiral cord.

"When's Mom coming home?'' Jason asked curiously.

"Apparently, whenever she likes.'' There was a cutting quality to Richard's reply. He was very, very annoyed. He had important research to do tonight, and instead he had to waste time foraging for dinner.

Jason watched the expression on his father's face, then volunteered enthusiastically, "I got an idea, Dad."

"What?"

"How about Chick-O-Rama fried chicken?" He waited for an answer. To Jason Avery, junk food was heaven.

"Fried chicken, huh?" Richard took one last look at the leg of lamb and flung it back inside the freezer. Then he reached for his car keys. "Let's hit the road, kid."

Fifteen minutes later, the two of them were standing at the counter of Chick-O-Rama, debating their dinner order with an acne-faced high school student.

"So, you want crunchy-crispy or super-crunchy-crispy?" the teenager inquired between pops of grape bubble gum.

This place, with its molded plastic chairs and square tables rooted to the floor, was certainly not the afterdeck of the S.S. *Charlie's Rubber Ducky*. The counterperson was no competition for Charlie Flagg's impeccable manservant, and the contrast made Richard more irritated than ever.

"What's the difference between crunchy-crispy and super-crunchy-crispy?" he asked at last.

The kid behind the Formica counter shrugged and blew a giant bubble. "Beats me. Chicken's chicken."

"If I were you," a soft, sexy and familiar voice said behind him, "I'd go for the crunchy-crispy. It's your best bet."

Richard turned around to get a full view

of Abby Cunningham. As always, the view was not a disappointment. She no longer wore that bewitching little dress from this morning. Instead, she was clad in baggy pants and a snug T-shirt that left little to the imagination. Of course, Abby could wear nothing but a burlap sack and still look delicious. Those incredible blue eyes seemed to be sending out more signals, and Richard had difficulty finding his voice. "You seem to be quite an aficionado." He forced himself to sound deliberately casual. "Come here often?"

Abby shrugged in the direction of Brian and Olivia, who were playfully pelting each other with plastic forks and straws at a nearby table. "The kids like it."

"Hey, Jason!" Brian yelled from his seat. "Why'd your dad bring you *here?* This place stinks!"

"My dad hates hamburgers, that's why!" Jason yelled back.

"Jason . . ." Richard looked at his son warningly, while Abby bit her lip in amusement.

Dark-haired Olivia Cunningham looked at Brian conspiratorially and gestured to Jason. "Hey, Jason, c'mere! Quick!" She pointed to one end of the table. "Look at this totally disgusting, gross bug!"

"Ooh, check it out!" Jason ran over enthusiastically. Going out to eat was such fun!

Abby focused her lovely eyes on Richard

again. "What *are* you doing here?" She
hesitated. "I mean, isn't Laura home
whipping up duck à l'orange or something? I hear she's a fabulous cook." Abby
learned everything she wanted to know
from Richard's significant pause.

"Laura's more interested in real estate
these days," he replied heavily.

Abby sighed with calculated wistfulness.
"I don't know anything about real estate."

Her words elicited the desired response
from Richard.

"Thank goodness for small favors," he
said glumly.

Abby paused. "I can't cook either." In
the distance, she could hear Olivia scream-
ing at Brian as her son attempted to
squash the giant bug. Despite the ruckus,
Abby kept a steady gaze on Richard. Right
now, it was terribly entertaining to banter
with him. She'd been so lonely and bored
recently. Richard Avery was one of the
few amusing men in the neighborhood,
and Abby was in need of some amusement. He was good-looking for his type
but a bit too boyish for Abby's usual taste,
and deciding what to do with Richard
Avery was not a matter that caused her
any loss of sleep. Sometimes Abby
thought it might be an interesting little
diversion; other times, she wondered if it
would be more trouble than it was worth.

Abby could feel Richard's eyes on the
clinging cotton material of her T-top, and

she enjoyed knowing that she held a subtle power over her neighbor. It was good
for her recently bruised ego. The interview
at Alcock's had been a total failure. Maybe
she should go work for her brother, Sid,
after all. If any place needed her skills as a
bookkeeper, it was Knots Landing Motors.
Besides, it might not be so bad to work in
the vicinity of that delightfully attractive
Gary Ewing. Abby certainly wanted to get
to know *him* better. Too bad he seemed so
devoted to his wife. Val and Gary Ewing
were almost as bad as Sid and Karen. She
disliked couples that appeared so damn
devoted to each other.

Of course, Abby realized it was all sour
grapes on her part. She'd never had a
truly satisfying relationship, perhaps
because she had never met a man she
could really respect. Take Richard Avery
here, standing in the middle of the Chick-
O-Rama with his tongue practically hanging out. It was almost a turn-off, but right
now, Richard Avery was about the best
Abby could do. The pickings in Knots
Landing were much leaner than Abby had
expected. She was beginning to question
whether moving there had been such a
great idea, after all. Well, she told herself,
it wasn't as if there had been any other
option. Jeff, her ex-husband, had left Abby
and the kids high and dry.

She pursed her lips and tried to shut her
delicate nostrils to the pungent odor of

greasy chicken. A moment later came another series of whoops and screams from the kids.

Richard squinted uncomfortably. "You really want to eat here?"

Abby cast a weary eye in the direction of Brian and Olivia, who were now engaged in a wrestling match for the ownership of the ketchup bottle. "I've been barred from most other restaurants in the area," she explained.

The teenager behind the counter popped another series of bubbles with his gum and rolled his eyes impatiently. "You folks gonna order or what?"

Abby's face brightened. "I have an idea. Why don't we join forces and have a picnic?"

"Your backyard or mine?" responded Richard instantly. This evening had taken a sudden turn for the better.

Abby lowered her voice ever so slightly. "Your backyard is . . . darker."

Richard swallowed and tried to conceal his excitement. "I think there's a bottle of Clos des Mouches in the refrigerator."

His sexy neighbor gave Richard another devastating smile. "That goes great with crunchy-crispy. Wouldn't you say?"

Richard wouldn't have minded if they'd been about to sit down to hot dogs and beer. In fact, in the sensual company of Abby Cunningham, he would gladly have eaten hamburgers.

* * *

Linda Striker looked up from Mrs. McGuane's car. She'd stayed late doing the repairs in the hope of setting her awful mistake right. Well, it wasn't the only reason. She wanted Sid Fairgate to see how conscientious she could be. She could only hope he'd notice. Right now, though, it was obvious, even from this distance, that the only thing Sid noticed was Gary Ewing's persistence. All afternoon, it seemed, the two men had been arguing about something. Right now, the senior partner of Knots Landing Motors seemed just about at the end of his tether.

"I don't want to talk about this anymore. It's late, and I've got to get home." Sid jangled the large ring of keys and continued to secure all the inner doors of the offices.

"I don't get what you're so uptight about," Gary continued to protest.

"That's obvious," Sid muttered. "I suppose a brick has to fall on your head in order for you to get the message."

Gary's hackles rose. "What's the big deal?" He refused to let up on Sid.

"I already told you. I don't want to discuss it right now." Sid reached for his sports jacket. He was tired of belaboring the issue with Ewing. All he wanted to do now was go home, eat a light dinner, hug his wife and then maybe shoot a few bas-

81

kets in the driveway with Eric and Michael. He enjoyed shooting baskets—it never failed to help him unwind. After a long day like this one, he sorely needed to do just that.

Gary followed him into the showroom. "You're being pretty stubborn about this, Sid."

"*I'm* being stubborn?"

Gary shook his head. "I don't get it, Sid. What's so strange about two guys starting up a cab company out here?"

"The guys," Sid answered tersely.

Linda watched as the two men started to walk out of the building. The idea of being left alone in the garage didn't thrill her, but she had no intention of leaving the job on Mrs. McGuane's axle half-finished. She had her pride. "Good night, Gary!" she called out. Then, keeping her voice as casual as possible, she added, "Good night, Mr. Fairgate!"

Sid stopped and turned around. He walked back in the direction of the service bay and looked at Mrs. McGuane's car, and then at Linda Striker's intense, grime-streaked young face. The kid really was trying, he was forced to admit. "Aren't you going home?"

Linda cast her eyes downward, trying to shake the tingling in her stomach because Sid was standing so close. "I'm almost finished," she said finally.

Her boss paused. In a more gentle voice,

he declared, "Okay. Just lock up after you leave."

"Sure." Linda hoped to heaven she wasn't blushing.

The icing on the cake was Sid's smile. "Good night, Linda."

"Good night," she replied softly and watched as the two men left the garage and walked toward the parking lot. After a moment, she picked up a wrench and started tightening a bolt. Damn, she wondered for the hundredth time today, why were all the really terrific men married?

Meanwhile, out in the parking lot, Gary continued to prod Sid. "I don't get it. Our business is selling cars. Their business is *their* business."

Sid slid into the driver's side and waited for Gary to get inside the car. He pressed his lips together thoughtfully. "Gary, I guess I don't look at it that way."

The other man waved his hand in the direction of the display area. "Look at it this way. You know how many of these gas guzzlers we've turned over in the past three months?"

"I *know* how many. You don't have to tell me." Sid started the engine and put the car in gear.

"Two, count 'em, two," Gary announced defiantly.

The older man backed the car into the traffic and looked straight ahead. "Let's talk about it tomorrow, huh?"

"Why can't we resolve this now?"

Sid was very tempted to put on the brakes but resisted the impulse. "I just want to do some checking."

"Checking?" Gary was mystified. "They're calling at nine! Have you checked with our accountant lately? Our sales dropped eighteen percent last month. That's seven points lower than the same quarter last year!" Gary couldn't believe his partner's negative attitude.

"I know the figures," Sid answered in a hard voice. In another minute, he was going to lean over and sock Gary Ewing in his stubborn jaw.

"Okay. You know, then, how much we need this sale! Korshak and Lance want fifteen cars! I honestly don't see why—"

Sid Fairgate almost ran a stop sign. "Don't push me, Gary!" He was ready to explode.

Gary was silent for a minute. "Look, Sid," he said slowly, "I don't see anybody else waiting in line for even one of those monsters! We need a sale like this. We need it badly. It could really put us back in business." His tone grew kinder. "Do you really believe we can afford to pass this opportunity up just because you don't like the color of their ties?"

Sid paused. "Gary, listen. I appreciate your enthusiasm, but let me tell you something. It so happens that I made a call this afternoon to the Better Business Bureau."

Gary's eyebrows shot up. "And?"

"And," Sid answered heavily, "according to them, there is no Orchid Cab and Delivery in Albuquerque, New Mexico."

And with that, the two men lapsed into an uneasy silence.

Out in the Avery backyard, the sun had gone down over an hour ago. The children were comfortably ensconced in the den watching television. Out on the patio table were strewn the sticky remnants of a Chick-O-Rama repast. In the yard, there was almost dead silence except for the chirping of a solitary cricket. In the shadows of the night, from inside the gazebo came the muted laughter of Richard and Abby. He poured each of them a refill of Clos des Mouches, enjoying the way Abby ran her slender, manicured fingers up and down the stem of the delicate wine goblet. He leaned back in the seat.

"A balmy, moonlit night, without a mosquito in sight, and our kids would rather be inside watching television," Richard observed.

Abby stretched her arms provocatively over her head. "They're too young to understand about moonlight." She moved a little closer to him on the summer couch. The wine made her feel so mellow and relaxed. Abby looked at Richard from out of the corner of her eye. He'd opened the

top few buttons of his shirt and she could
see the dark hairs curling on his upper
chest. She had never really noticed before
how well built he was. The old dungarees
he now wore accentuated his lean hips
and long legs. It had been an hour since
Richard Avery had discarded his shoes.
Abby waited a moment, then remarked
casually, "It must be difficult for Jason."

Richard looked up from his glass. "Difficult? What do you mean?"

Abby shook her head sympathetically.
"You know, with Laura working and all."

"Oh, right." He nodded in agreement
and gulped another mouthful of wine.

Abby closed in on the target. "Of
course, it can't be too easy on *you*, either."

Richard sighed. "I don't mind the idea
of Laura working, don't get me wrong—"

"Of course not," Abby agreed quickly.

"But it's starting to affect things at
home, if you know what I mean."

"Sure I do." Abby's big blue eyes
misted over understandingly.

She's quite a woman, Richard thought.
Quite a woman. But aloud he said,
"Y'know what I'm saying, Abby. I
wouldn't care about this second-career
thing, only she's gotten so obsessed about
it. Almost downright *fanatical!*"

Abby leaned a little closer and took careful, deliberate aim. "I don't think both
parents should work." Her voice was
almost coy. "When I was married, I didn't

work. For me, the man has to be the dominant one.'' Sure, she thought. That's where the trouble started. Jeff always wanting *her* to make the decisions. It was as if he were looking for another mother. Well, Abby had no intention of being on the receiving end of some poor guy's Oedipus complex. She didn't want to be the boss in the relationship. She wanted a man who could take care of her, not just financially, but in *every* way. Particularly in bed.

''Sometimes Laura tries to be bossy,'' Richard said. ''You know, she insists a thing's got to be done *her* way. It really gets on my nerves.'' He poured Abby a little more wine.

''I was married so young,'' she said wistfully. ''I'd never been, you know, with a man before.''

Richard almost dropped the bottle. It was pretty difficult trying to picture Abby Cunningham as a virgin.

The lovely woman sighed. ''It was a disaster, really. We weren't sexually compatible.'' She looked up meaningfully. ''I think that's really important, don't you?''

Richard tried not to spill his wine down the front of his shirt. ''Oh, absolutely.'' He paused. ''It's the one thing with Laura and me that's solid.'' Recently? Who was he kidding? But he'd never admit that to anyone, particularly Abby Cunningham. It would hardly be a glowing testimonial, and he felt an urgent desire to impress her.

Abby ran her tongue thoughtfully over her lower lip. "Are there a lot of men in the office where she works?"

Richard nodded. "Yeah. Her boss is a guy named Scooter Warren." At Abby's question, he felt his preserves being threatened. That Warren was slick and smooth-talking. Was it possible that Laura was interested in him as more than an employer?

"He's married, isn't he?" Abby fired at her target, and hit a bull's-eye.

"Yeah," Richard replied. He pressed his lips together. "How about some more wine?"

Abby nodded pleasantly. "Mmmm. Sounds heavenly." She waited for him to fill her glass once more and then purred, "I never realized, Richard . . ."

He looked up, curiously. "Realized what?"

"Why, you have so much hair on your chest." She leaned over provocatively. "I suppose I never really noticed before 'cause I've never actually seen you without your shirt on."

Richard smiled in obvious pleasure and moved just a little closer himself. "Tell me more," he murmured, "I'm all ears."

Laura Avery entered the front hallway and noticed the light coming from the direction of the den. She was puzzled as she caught the high-pitched sound of childish laughter. Still carrying her portfolio, she walked toward the den. There she saw Jason and the two Cunningham kids, Olivia and Brian, munching on a bowl of popcorn and staring with glazed eyes at the television screen. From the screeching brakes and whining sirens, Laura assumed it was the typical police-chase movie. She kissed Jason affectionately. "You kids are up late," she said good-naturedly. "Where's your daddy?"

Jason looked up belatedly. "Oh, hi, Mom."

"Where's Daddy?" Laura repeated.

Olivia Cunningham stared at the television, blindly reaching for a handful of popcorn. "They're outside . . . drinking wine."

Laura stood there. "They?" Who exactly was "they"? She slowly put her portfolio down against the leg of the table and walked over to the sliding doors leading out onto the patio. She stepped outside and looked around in the tranquil darkness. Then she heard laughter from the gazebo, and her mouth tightened. Laura took a few steps closer. There was more laughter.

"Richard?" she called out tentatively.

There was a long pause. "We're over here," he answered finally.

Laura walked toward the gazebo and

then she saw them. Richard and Abby Cunningham. Sitting so close together on the couch they were practically touching. Each of them holding a wine glass. An empty wine bottle was lying on the gazebo floor, catching the glint of the moonlight. Richard without shoes, his shirt unbuttoned practically to his navel. As usual when she was flustered, Laura began to babble. ''Uh, hi, Abby.''

Abby smiled as if she were a party to the world's most amusing inside joke. ''Hi there, Laura.''

Laura simply didn't know what to do except to continue to babble as if the sight of her husband practically in the arms of the neighborhood vamp was the most normal thing on earth. ''Uh, we sold that house today in the Palisades, and Scooter insisted we celebrate with a client . . . and drinks just turned into dinner.'' She paused. ''I called but there was no answer.''

Richard exchanged glances with Abby. ''What did you eat?''

Laura shrugged. ''What did I eat? Oh, cold salmon with mousseline sauce.''

Her husband didn't look at her. ''We had chicken from Chick-O-Rama.''

Laura felt her temper simmering. ''At least you weren't alone.''

Abby Cunningham stood up, looking as slender and lovely as ever. She patted Laura on the arm. ''If you'd gotten here sooner, you could've joined us.''

Laura smiled tightly, resisting the urge to kick her beautiful neighbor right in her little behind.

Less than an hour later, Laura stood in the kitchen, emptying the last of the paper plates into the trash basket. Suddenly Richard entered the room, dressed in a suit and tie. Laura looked up in astonishment. ''Honey, where are you going?''

Richard ignored her and walked over to the coffee maker. He methodically reached for a large thermos bottle and poured in the hot contents. Silently, he twisted the lid shut and set the thermos down on the counter.

''Richard?'' Laura asked again, with growing alarm.

Slowly, he turned to her. ''I lost half a day because of you, Laura.''

''Because of *me?*'' Laura untied the strings of her appliqué apron and stared at him in puzzlement.

''I have to go back and work in the library.'' The reply was curt.

''I'm really sorry—'' Laura was apologetic ''—but I sold my first house today. Well, I didn't exactly sell it legally, because I'm not licensed yet. But I'm responsible for the sale.'' She waited for a comment, congratulations, anything. There was just dead silence. ''Isn't that exciting?''

Richard yawned. ''Thrilling.''

Laura walked toward him and put a conciliatory arm around him. With her other hand, she began lovingly to caress her husband's face. "Honey, couldn't you just get up a little earlier instead of going out now? I haven't seen you all day. We haven't had any time to talk." She hesitated. "I missed you."

Richard shrugged indifferently. "I've got a hearing at ten in the morning. If I don't come up with something we can use, Arkansas Gas and Fuel isn't going to get their easement." He pulled away from her embrace, picked up his thermos and walked over to get his briefcase.

Laura stood there, uncertain. "Wake me up when you get home. I don't care what time it is."

He didn't even look in her direction. "I probably won't *be* home."

Unhappily, she twisted her fingers together. "I feel terrible about this, Richard." Her voice was tremulous. "It won't happen again, I promise."

"No," said Richard tonelessly, checking his wristwatch, "it won't." He walked out of the kitchen and headed straight for the front door. When he reached it, he turned around, as if for effect, and remarked, "That's great about the house. You seem to have a real flair for real estate." His lip curled slightly. "I'm sure you'll be successful wherever you are." He turned around and opened the door.

Laura stared after him. "What do you mean?" she asked slowly.

Richard jiggled his car keys. "When you see that boss of yours tomorrow, ask him to recommend some brokers in Chicago."

"Chicago? Why Chicago?" Laura followed her husband down the front steps into the driveway.

Richard tossed his keys in the air and deftly caught them. "Because that's where we're moving." He didn't wait for Laura's stunned reply but simply continued on to his car.

Chapter Six
Rude Awakening

At first, Karen didn't hear a thing. She was far too lost in the most wonderful dream. It was a bright, California afternoon and the sun was glittering down on the blue waves of the Pacific. It was just the two of them, on their very own sailboat, floating deliciously across the water. Sid leaned across the deck to hand her a tall glass of iced tea with a fresh mint sprig. As she reached for the frosty glass, Karen's eyes scanned her husband's tanned, muscular chest with open admiration. And Sid's eyes were appreciating his wife's sun-bronzed body, clad in the skimpiest of bikinis. It made Karen feel sexy and beautiful, warm and desired.

"It's so wonderful to get away, just the two of us," Sid murmured in a low growl.

"Perfect, darling," she whispered happily. Karen was never more in love with her husband than at this very moment. Their fingers briefly brushed against each other as she took the iced tea from Sid's hand.

Suddenly, the wet glass slipped from her grasp and fell onto the deck of the sailboat, shattering into a hundred pieces. Strangely, the splintering sound did not come from the crashing of the glass onto the deck, but from far, far away. At once the dream dissolved, and Karen awoke abruptly. She sat up in bed with a start, her ears suddenly alert. The noise had come from downstairs. In the silence of the night, Karen could distinctly hear even more sounds. There were several thuds and another crash. Something was definitely going on downstairs. Panicked, she leaned over to her sleeping husband. Bless Sid's heart, she thought with a curious blend of fear and cynicism, he could sleep through a typhoon.

"Sid!" Hastily, she shook his shoulder. He didn't even budge. "Sid!" Her raspy whisper grew louder. From below their room, there came another thud. Now fully awakened and alert, Karen was cold with fear. Intruders in her home! Burglars, or worse! In the space of a few seconds, a hundred horrifying thoughts shot through her mind. Let the burglars take everything—the silverware from the oak hutch, the television set, the stereo system in the den—just let them stay downstairs!

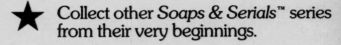
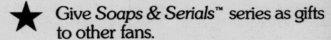
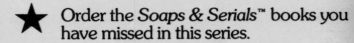

You can now order previous titles of *Soaps & Serials*™ Books by mail!

Just complete the order form, detach, and send together with your check or money order payable to:

Soaps & Serials™
120 Brighton Road, Box 5201
Clifton, NJ 07015-5201

- - - - - - - - - - - - - - - - - -

Please <u>circle</u> the book #'s you wish to order:

The Young and The Restless	1	2	3	4	5	6	7	8
Days of Our Lives	1	2	3	4	5	6	7	8
Guiding Light	1	2	3	4	5	6	7	8
Another World	1	2	3	4	5	6	7	8
As The World Turns	1	2	3	4	5	6	7	8
Dallas™	1	2	3	4	5	6	7	8
Knots Landing™	1	2	3	4	5	6	7	8
Capitol™	1	2	3	4	NOT AVAILABLE			

Each book is $2.50 ($3.50 in Canada).

Total number of books
circled _____ × price above = $ _____

Sales tax (CT and NY residents only) $ _____

Shipping and Handling $ _____ .95

Total payment enclosed $ _____
(check or money orders only)

Name _____

Address _____ Apt# _____

City _____

State _____ Zip _____

Telephone (_____) _____
   Area code

KL 8

Let them take whatever they came for and leave. She thought of her three children, sleeping peacefully in their bedrooms, and felt a mother's terror for the safety of her babies.

"Sid, wake up!" She gave her husband one final, sharp nudge.

"Huh?" He stirred at last and stared at her with sleep-glazed eyes.

"Downstairs!" Karen whispered, her tone urgent.

Sid, at first disappointed at being unceremoniously torn from the most wonderful dream—about his car engine winning the Indy 500—was immediately wide awake. The fear in his wife's voice washed the last vestiges of sleep from him. "Honey," he questioned, "what is it?"

"Downstairs!" Karen repeated. "Listen."

Sid could hear the footsteps in the living room. Without another moment's hesitation, he threw the covers back. Careful not to make a sound, he slid from the bed and drew in his breath sharply. "Stay here. I'm going down to check it out."

"No way," Karen shot back. "I'm right behind you!" She followed her husband as he gingerly opened the bedroom door and headed toward the top of the landing.

Sharply, Sid gestured for Karen to remain behind him, and they began to creep slowly down the stairs.

God, Karen prayed, *let there be only one*

burglar. Please, don't let him have a gun.
Another paralyzing thought: *What if the man or men had a switchblade?*

Sid, who was several steps ahead of his wife, was thinking almost the same thing. Part of him was sick with fear, but a stubbornness kept him moving toward the living room. Stronger than fear was the emotion of outrage. How dare anyone disturb the sanctity of his home? Without pausing to consider the consequences, he reached for the switch on the wall, immediately flooding the room with bright light. The unwelcome intruder stood revealed. It was not a hulking felon but an adolescent boy in a pair of blue pajamas.

"Michael?" Karen gasped, staring at her younger son in disbelief. The boy continued to walk around the room, in a series of circles.

"Son?" Sid stepped forward, confused.

Michael stopped dead in his tracks and blinked. What were his parents doing on the staircase, staring down at him as if he were some kind of Martian? He squinted. His older brother, Eric, and big sister Diana were staring down at him, too, over their parents' shoulders. What was wrong with everybody, anyhow? He scratched his blond head sleepily. Perplexed, he took a step toward the landing. "What's wrong?" he asked, puzzled. "What are you guys all staring at?"

Sid turned to look at Karen, who could

only shake her head numbly in complete bafflement.

At the breakfast table that morning, Sid acted as if nothing had happened, Karen thought irritably. He sat there, completely absorbed in his bacon and scrambled eggs. "Honey," she continued to probe, "doesn't it worry you?"

He gave a shrug. "Kids sleepwalk all the time." And reached for another slice of toast.

Karen pursed her lips and refilled both of their mugs with fragrant, fresh-brewed coffee. But this morning, she didn't pause to appreciate its rich, mellow taste. "It wasn't sleepwalking," she replied evenly.

Sid knew that tone in her voice only too well, and set down his knife and fork. "Sweetheart, I think you're making too much of this."

"He wasn't sleeping," Karen insisted. "Couldn't you see that? He was wide awake, walking around in circles . . . in the dark!"

Sid glanced idly at his cuff links. "How can you say the kid was awake? It was four o'clock in the morning, Karen."

"I know," she replied in a low voice.

Sid looked at the deep concern etched in his wife's face and placed a gentle hand on her shoulder. "Be realistic, Karen. Why *would* Michael be awake at such an ungodly hour?"

Karen shook her head. "I can't answer that, Sid, and that's what worries me."

Sid removed his hand and announced assertively, "There's nothing to worry yourself about. He was just sleepwalking, and that's all there is to it."

"You're wrong, Dad." The voice came from the other side of the kitchen. Eric Fairgate, dressed in his best blue jeans, shoved an unruly lock of hair away from his eyes. "Michael wasn't sleepwalking. I mean, he was awake."

"What are you talking about?" Karen said, her voice no more than a whisper.

Her elder son shrugged and reached for an apple from the fruit bowl. "He does it all the time, Mom."

"Does what?" she asked tersely.

The teenager rubbed the red apple against the soft material of his sweater until it was shiny. "You know, he gets up . . . walks around."

Sid hesitated. "Haven't you asked him why he does it?"

Eric gave a deep yawn and regarded both parents coolly. "Yeah, I asked him . . . of course I asked him. He says he doesn't know." There was a long, uncomfortable silence in the room.

Eric's eyes flickered back and forth between his mother and father. You could cut the tension in the kitchen with a knife, that's how thick it was. He thought, with a typical teenage sense of superiority, that adults weren't all that sharp. He and his sister, Diana, had been aware of their younger brother's weird nocturnal ramblings for quite some time. It was difficult to believe that their parents were only *now* hip to Michael's nighttime habits.

"See you later!" He gave them both a quick wave and rushed out the door, already ten minutes late for school.

Karen felt smothered by the silence in the kitchen. "Sid . . ." she began uncertainly.

He smiled at her with forced brightness. "Karen, he was fine this morning." There was another long pause. He'd been married to Karen too long not to recognize the significance of such a pause. "Relax, honey." But he knew she hardly heard him. "Relax," he repeated once more and then reached for the sports section of the morning paper.

Karen bit her lower lip thoughtfully and stared into her half-empty coffee mug. "Relax? Sure, I'll relax. In fact, maybe I'll just do a couple of laps in the living room!"

Sid gave a laugh and buried his head back in the sports pages.

Karen sat quietly, across the table, but she might as well have been across the ocean. She could only think of Michael and his bizarre behavior. Something was wrong, and she hadn't the faintest idea what it was.

* * *

Mrs. Janet Crane, the art instructor at Knots Landing Junior High School, prided herself on being part of the "new wave" of education. Only thirty-two years old, she still felt like the long-haired pixie who had graduated from Cooper Union in New York City nearly ten years ago. Since that time, she'd watched as her classmates became successful artists and photographers—some of them had carved out spectacular niches in the world of advertising. They had either talent or drive, or both. Janet had neither, and she accepted this fact. She subscribed to the old adage "Those who can—do, and those who can't—teach." Only when learning of an old college friend's success did something within her heart cry out for the lost dream, but such aches occurred less frequently these days. She truly loved teaching, and found working with young people refreshing. They lacked the pretensions of older students. Today, for example, she observed the two sharply contrasting styles of Eddie Wilson and Michael Fairgate. Both boys were creative and filled with energy, yet, looking at the paintings on their easels, she was struck by the violence of Michael's work. It was abstract and vividly colored. In fact, the boy's use of strong, clashing hues almost gave the teacher a headache. She turned away from the bright reds and oranges and rested her eyes briefly on a soothing still life painted in mild pink and white tones on another student's canvas; peaceful, yes, but unimaginative, she thought.

As Janet Crane turned her head away, Michael began to shift restlessly from one foot to the other. He wasn't sure if he bumped into Eddie on purpose or by accident. All he knew was that he suddenly shoved against his schoolmate hard enough to make him spill some of his paint.

"Hey!" Eddie complained. "Watch out, will you?"

"Watch out yourself" was Michael's surly reply. He knew it was his fault, but some contrary imp inside him wouldn't stop. Suddenly, he was irritated for no particular reason, and Eddie Wilson seemed to be a bigger nerd than he usually was. Yeah, a real nerd.

His opinion of Eddie was confirmed when the other boy glanced with deprecation at his painting. "What's that, huh?"

Michael looked at him disdainfully. "None of your business." *Nerd!*

"It's weird," Eddie shot back. "I mean, *really* weird."

Without hesitating, Michael lowered his brush into paint and drew an ugly streak across the other boy's picture.

"You asked for it, Fairgate!" Eddie cried, and with his own dripping brush, he smeared an angry path across Michael's canvas. Seconds later, it had escalated into a full-fledged paint fight, with the other children in the room noisily cheering.

Oh, not again, thought Janet Crane wearily, as she rushed across the room to separate the two battling adolescents. "Stop it! Stop it now!" she ordered briskly.

Almost in a defiant whine, Eddie Wilson declared, "*He* started it, Mrs. Crane!" Immediately, several of the other children chimed in their agreement. It was obvious whose side most of them were on.

This incident was not a great surprise to Janet Crane. Just what had gotten into the Fairgate boy recently? She stared at him quietly and then sighed. "Again, Michael?" But the boy didn't reply. He simply stood there, the dripping paintbrush still tightly grasped in his fingers. And then he gave his teacher a curiously indifferent shrug.

Laura Avery, dressed immaculately as ever, rang the front doorbell and waited for Karen's invitation to come in.

"Hey, neighbor," Karen asked from her comfortable position on the floor, "do you know anything about plants?" A big book was cradled in her lap.

"Plants, huh?" Laura smiled back. "I can say with complete assurance that I know absolutely nothing about plants. If they survive in my house it's only because they've mastered the art of actually watering themselves," she said, chuckling.

Karen grinned, inwardly musing at her neighbor's perfect appearance. From the exquisitely coiffed red hair to the elegant wool suit, Laura Avery always looked as if she'd just stepped down from a bandbox. If her husband was too dumb to appreciate her, more the fool he. But aloud, she merely remarked, "I've got this real sick one," and pointed to a pitiful plant by the window. "I can't decide whether it's mealy bugs or aphids—" Karen hunched thoughtfully over on her elbows "—on the other hand, it might be African root rot." It was quite obvious that Laura was only half-listening. She seemed quite distracted this morning.

"Hey," Karen offered cheerfully, "you know what I'll do with this uncooperative green creature? I'll simply give it two aspirin and put it to bed!" She laughed at her own joke, and realized that Laura wasn't laughing, not even a minimal laugh of forced politeness. All she could manage was a faint smile. Karen rose from her cross-legged position and brushed the dirt from her hands. "You don't seem so well yourself, Laura," she murmured. "Are you okay?"

"I guess," Laura replied unconvincingly. "Yes . . . no." She threw her head back. "Oh, I don't know!"

"That covers all the bases," Karen observed. "So, what's wrong?"

Laura sighed. ''I wanted to talk to you about Richard. And Abby.''

''Oh,'' Karen replied in a noncommittal tone. She was uncomfortable when women asked her for an opinion on spouses with a roving eye. It reminded Karen only too clearly of high school, when girlfriends would want to know if the boys they were crazy about had *really* been necking with somebody else at last night's party. Karen was not a busybody by nature, and she simply didn't want to say anything that might cause distress to her obviously vulnerable neighbor.

''About Richard and Abby.'' Laura began to pace the room distractedly. ''Have you noticed anything between them?''

''Between them?'' Karen repeated vaguely.

''Sometimes I think it's an act to make me feel bad,'' she continued more to herself than to Karen, ''and sometimes I think they're actually having an affair.'' She waited for a response from Karen.

''Have you talked to Richard?'' The other woman tried to steer the subject away from the obvious.

''No.'' Laura nervously shifted from one high-heeled shoe to the other. Damn, she hated being so exposed, so vulnerable! She could almost feel Karen's unspoken pity. What she had come here for was just a chance to talk to someone else about her worst fears. "I guess I wanted to verbalize my feelings with another person." She brushed an imaginary stray hair out of her moist eye. "I just wanted to discover if I might be imagining things."

Karen truly did not know what to say to her friend. How could she, in any conscience, tell Laura what was on her mind? Did she have any right to contribute to the poor woman's distress by feeding more suspicions onto the flames? She still did not have the faintest idea whether or not Abby Cunningham had gotten her superbly manicured claws into her latest object of prey just yet, but it was obvious that Richard and his sexy neighbor were playing some kind of dangerous game. They flirted with each other openly and carelessly, while poor Laura stood by and watched. It was almost a relief when the phone rang shrilly and shattered the awkward silence. Karen rushed to answer it, eager for the opportunity to escape Laura's queries.

As Karen spoke in quiet, terse tones on the phone, Laura stared unhappily out the picture window. Somehow, she was unable to free her mind of the image of Abby Cunningham snuggling up against Richard in the gazebo. All this was compounded by Richard's bewildering outburst of the night before. Was he truly serious about moving to Chicago? It seemed so far out in left field, he must have been kidding. On the other hand, she considered, staring out onto the perfectly mowed lawn, maybe it would take a two-thousand-mile move to keep Abby away from her husband. Laura wondered if it was worth the trouble.

Just then Karen set the telephone receiver down and came back into the living room, looking highly agitated.

"Could we talk about this later? I've got to drive over to the school."

Laura stepped away from the window and noticed the new tension on her neighbor's face. "Michael?" she asked briefly.

Karen sighed. "Again." She glanced around the room for her purse.

For just an instant, Laura forgot the problems weighing heavily on her own heart and felt a wave of pity for Karen. "Sure. Go ahead. We can talk later." She waved her hand as Karen fumbled for the car keys. In another moment, the two of them were out the door.

Richard Avery dozed against a pile of dusty law volumes. His clothes were rumpled, and everywhere was strewn the debris of his all-night research session at the office library. Pencils, worn down to the nub, dozens of files, legal pads and the remains of numerous Styrofoam coffee cups cluttered the long, sleek wood table.

Millie, the receptionist, entered the room that morning and stared in amazement at the sleeping attorney. "Hey, Richard!" She reached over and tapped his shoulder. Good heavens, the man had been here all night. "Oh, excuse me, Sleeping Beauty—" she continued to shake him "—but this is your wake-up call! You've got that hearing at ten o'clock with Cargill, remember?"

Richard stirred and stared up at her with glazed eyes. "Yeah, right," he finally mumbled, "just dozing off for a minute, that's all." He gave a huge yawn and stretched out his arms in a grand gesture. He couldn't help but brag, even to this receptionist from New York. "Got some great stuff," he murmured, "dynamite stuff! We're going to mow those guys down, let me tell you!" His head still swam groggily with visions of his intense research—the statistics on Indian fishing rights, jurisdictional disputes and water ordinances. "We're going to knock them right on their butts!"

Millie, who had the benefits of a full night's sleep and a freshening shower, could only nod her head agreeably and wonder how this ambitious young lawyer was going to manage to look presentable enough for a day at court. With his stubble of a beard and disheveled hair, he resembled a businessman who had just completed a twenty-four-hour bus trip. What a mess! She found his jacket slung carelessly over one of the leather chairs and helped him into it. Something about Richard Avery always brought out the mother in Millie, even though she was more than ten years his junior.

"You'd better believe it," Richard was saying aloud, his voice alive with confidence. He held up a book. "Here's a case where the Indians lost. *Kwakiutl Federation* versus *Sacramento Power and Light*." There was a pause. "All this environmental litigation at the tip of my fingers!"

"That's wonderful," the young woman mused vaguely, wondering where on earth she could find a comb for him.

Richard wanted to perform a tap dance, he was so delighted with himself this morning. "Millie, I'm handing this case to Cargill on a silver platter. All he has to do is serve it."

"Mmm," the girl responded, "that's terrific. Meanwhile, you might want to try washing up. You don't exactly look as fresh as a daisy right now, and everyone's going to be here any minute." She'd better get this guy a cup of strong coffee and clear the film away from his bloodshot eyes. Aloud she muttered, "If Simpson sees you like this . . ."

Richard wanted to laugh at the faint disapproval in her tone. "Simpson can stick it in his ear for all I care!" As soon as the words were out of his mouth, he realized they were true. Never before, at any moment during his time at Pincus, Simpson and Lyle, had his heart been filled with more antagonism toward his employers. Those overbearing, self-righteous egotists, always looking down their Ivy League noses at him. Well, today Richard Avery was going to show them a thing or two.

"This is my swan song, baby," Richard informed a stupefied Millie. "When this case is over, I'm hitching my train to the King of Torts and moving east!" There, he'd said it aloud, and it sounded marvelous. It had an almost noble ring.

"On second thought," the receptionist replied dubiously, "how about a black coffee with a double scotch?"

Richard bestowed one of his more beneficent smiles. "I'm not kidding. Cargill offered me a job."

Millie stared back at him doubtfully. She had been raised in one of the toughest areas of New York City, and the streetwise cynicism had never left her heart. "What kind of job?"

Richard glowed. "In Chicago. With him. If we beat the postponement."

Millie sighed. She had met many men like Lynn Baker Cargill in her relatively short life. Millie had struggled to support herself through secretarial school and had worked hard her entire twenty-five years. She was a pragmatist and never allowed herself to be impressed by a smooth-talking man, particularly any man who used the expression "trust me." Aloud, she said gently, "Richard, Cargill's got a reputation for making promises he—"

"He told me yesterday," Richard interrupted with childish insistence, "on Flagg's yacht. He told me I was too good a lawyer for this firm."

The young woman sighed. Why should she play the heavy in this discussion, anyhow? Richard Avery had the look of a child who was being asked to give up his favorite toy. "Look," she said in her most conciliatory tone, "I'm not disagreeing with you, but if I were in your shoes, I'd make damn sure I had a definite offer before I burned my bridges and hopped a plane for Chicago."

Richard stared back at her with unforgiving eyes. "You getting me that coffee or not?"

Millie shrugged and headed toward the door. She practically collided with Simpson and Cargill. "Oh, good morning, Mr. Cargill!" Speaking of the devil, she thought wryly. "Morning, Mr. Simpson."

Simpson gave her the usual perfunctory nod he reserved for the lowliest of his employees. "Millie." His cold blue eyes observed the attorney standing all rumpled before him. "Mr. Avery—" he now used his strictest, displeased schoolmaster voice "—you've kept Mr. Cargill waiting. There's a car downstairs."

A few days ago, Richard might have

been shivering in his shoes. Now it was all he could do not to look at his boss with complete disdain. To Richard's complete delight, L. B. Cargill walked over to the long table and regarded the wreckage of the all-night research session.

"Looks like it was all for a good cause," he observed with a smile.

"There's a lot of Havana cigars at stake." Richard grinned back. It was gratifying to note the look of total confusion on Simpson's face, like a man being left out of an inside joke.

"Cigars?" was all the senior partner could murmur blankly.

Cargill winked at Richard conspiratorially, then said, "Give him a raise, Simpson, or I'm liable to stick him in my trunk and lug him back to Chicago."

Richard noted Simpson's uneasy laugh. "I did dig up a few things," he said directly to Cargill, ignoring his own boss completely.

"Enough to hold them off at the pass?"

"Enough to blow 'em clean out of the water!" Richard's voice oozed confidence.

"In that case, Richard," Cargill gestured toward the door, "let's not keep them waiting." Ignoring the stunned expressions on Millie's and Simpson's faces, Richard exited the room with Cargill and departed for the Coastal Commission hearing in a cloud of glory.

Chapter Seven

Secret Strategies

The three of them were sitting in an automobile parked on one of Knots Landing's more deserted streets. Roy Lance, Frank Korshak and Gary Ewing. Gary hadn't told Sid about his decision to meet with the two businessmen. Some things, he reflected, a person had to do on his own instinct. Right now, his Ewing instinct for making money was operating full throttle. And he *did* have that Ewing instinct—he was born with it, despite what his older brother, J.R., chose to believe. Gary craved that instant gratification, that rush to his ego, and for this reason he had agreed to meet surreptitiously with Roy and Frank. He resented Sid's plodding, methodical way of doing business. He wanted the chance to prove that he, Gary Ewing, could take control and make a deal on his own steam. Right now, it seemed to him that Orchid Cab and Delivery was a perfect way to show that he knew a good deal when he saw one.

And he *was* right, thought Gary with gratification, as he looked first at the burly Frank Korshak and then at the collegiate partner, Roy Lance. Roy was droning on in that cultured prep school voice of his. "We went over the figures last night." He paused significantly. "We'd like to do business, Gary, but eight and a half percent is our bottom line."

Gary looked at both men with practiced calm. "Don't take this the wrong way, gentlemen, but Sid called the Better Business Bureau in Albuquerque—" he made a careful note of the unchanging expression on both men's faces "—and there's no listing for Orchid Cab and Delivery." He waited for a response.

Suddenly, there was a low chuckle from Roy. "Orchid's the *company* name," he explained patiently. "Wherever we're franchised we use the name of the state flower." He exchanged quick glances with his partner. "In Albuquerque, we're registered as Yucca Cab and Delivery. The yucca is New Mexico's state flower." He examined a carefully groomed fingernail. "Bet you didn't know that, did you, Gary?"

Gary's mental wheels were turning swiftly, "So—" he worked it out thoughtfully "—if Sid wanted to check credit refer-

ences, financial records, that sort of thing
. . . he'd ask about Yucca Cab and Delivery in Albuquerque, am I right?''

Roy nodded smoothly. ''And in Denver,
Columbia Cab—in Phoenix, Saguaro Cab—
Tulsa, mistletoe—''

Frank coughed and interrupted his partner. ''He trusts you, doesn't he, Gary?''

''You mean Sid?''

Frank leaned back against the velour
headrest and pressed his hard lips
together. ''In fact, maybe *you're* the one to
make those inquiries.''

There was a significant silence, and Gary
could notice the quick glances the other
two men exchanged. ''You might have a
point,'' he said slowly, ''but what if he
wants to look at the books?''

Frank Korshak, a man not known for
smiling, suddenly graced Gary Ewing with
a dazzling smile. ''We got nothing to
hide,'' he stated with supreme confidence,
''nothing to hide at all.''

Linda was working on a car with Sid,
watching every move he made with an
almost worshipful expression on her face.
He was such an intense person, so filled
with a contained vitality. Especially in this
confined area, underneath a car jacked up
on the hydraulic lift, Linda felt like a
tongue-tied schoolgirl, just being so close
to her boss. The way his lean, rangy figure
looked in those coveralls, that streak of

grime across his incredibly masculine pro-
file. Linda swallowed involuntarily. This
was absurd, having a teenage crush on Sid
Fairgate. But she was terrified of saying
something stupid that might reveal her
vulnerability. How mortifying if he discovered her feelings too soon. Maybe he
already knew, she thought and suddenly
panicked. Maybe he could tell just by looking at her face, and the way she lowered
her eyes self-consciously when he looked
at her for just a split second too long.
God, and here she was, trying to prove
herself in a man's domain, the last bastion
of male chauvinism, an automobile garage.
She bit her lip decisively—it was hard
enough getting accepted as one of the
mechanics, she couldn't risk it all by
behaving like a simpering female.

"Hand me that wrench, will you?" Sid's
voice interrupted her thoughts.

Jarred back to reality, Linda silently
obeyed Sid's command and stared at him
with undisguised admiration. Could he see
it in her eyes? Quickly, desperately, she
searched for something to say to dispel her
inner tensions. "Uh, I hear you made a
fleet deal with some big cab company."
With satisfaction, she noted Sid's ears perk
up with interest. "Gary said we had fifteen cars to prep by Tuesday."

Sid's eyes narrowed. "What?"

"Sure," Linda continued, oblivious of
Sid's tension, "he asked me and some of

the boys if we had any time over the weekend." It was at that moment Linda noticed the muscle in Sid's jaw and the hard set of his mouth. "Mr. Fairgate?" she asked tentatively. But it was too late, she was talking to air. Sid was already striding purposefully toward his office. Bewildered, Linda watched as her boss gestured angrily to Gary Ewing, motioning for him to step outside the glass partition. What was all this about? the young woman wondered. Why was Sid so annoyed? Had she put her foot in her mouth again?

Sid was glaring at Gary with unconcealed rage. "Who told you to prep those cars?"

Gary put up his hands and smiled back at Sid. "Would you just listen?"

Sid tried to control his anger. He could barely believe that Gary could go behind his back like this. He could tell by the pleased expression on the young Texan's face that he thought he was doing Knots Landing Motors a fabulous favor. Sid fought for control. Sid took a deep breath. "Gary," he said with forced calm, "we haven't closed this deal and we're not going to close it until—"

"Sid—" Gary smiled again, showing his perfect, white All-American teeth "—I called my cousin in Albuquerque. He works for the government. You know, the Federal Task Force on Organized Crime?" He waited, and just as expected, his words were having a mollifying effect on his partner. "These guys may *look* funny but they're not connected. They run a small, efficient operation that in ten months is already giving the established companies some serious competition." With satisfaction, he noticed the harshness in Sid's features begin to soften. "As for a financial statement, Roy says it's already in the mail. Independent audit."

Sid gave a long sigh. "Why didn't you tell me this before?"

"I didn't want you to know till now," replied Gary honestly.

Somewhere, in the back of Sid's mind, the warning bells were ringing. "Gary," he began tentatively.

Gary's voice suddenly turned defensive and challenging. "Hey, what's the matter, Sid? Don't you trust me?"

"Sure I trust you," the other man said with a sigh. "It's just that . . ." How could he explain to Gary about his inner doubts? How could he hope for someone as brash and headstrong as Gary to understand his own reticence to enter into any kind of deal that seemed almost too good to be true?

"Why are you giving me the third degree, then?" Gary probed, almost indignantly.

Sid ran a hand through his rumpled hair. "No third degree. I just . . ." He was unable to complete the sentence. At this moment, despite all his instincts about Frank Korshak and Roy Lance, he wasn't sure what he felt anymore.

Gary sensed Sid's ambivalence. "Sid," he pleaded gently, "won't you trust me on this?"

Sid sighed again. He was so tired, tired of arguments, tired of being the heavy— just plain tired. "Gary, it's not that I don't trust you . . . it's just that there is never a time when a person can be too careful."

Gary smiled persuasively. "I'm not arguing with that, Sid, but, like I said—do me a favor and trust me, okay?"

Sid gave a resigned shrug and nodded unhappily. It wasn't as if he had much of a choice. The deed was already done, he thought glumly.

From the corner of her eye, Karen watched her son shift restlessly in his chair in the outer office. Michael was upset, and it didn't help to have his mother called to school so that this unpleasant guidance counselor could tell her all the things she thought were wrong with him. Michael thrust his hands in his pockets and tried to ignore the annoyance on Karen's face as she sat waiting for the guidance counselor to get off the telephone. Abruptly, Michael thrust his hands in the pockets of his jeans and stood up. He started to pace the floor of the office until he noticed an angry look on his mother's face. It was enough to subdue him for a moment. Obediently he returned to his chair.

Karen sighed wearily and twisted her lips in annoyance. How long did this guidance counselor expect her to keep waiting? She'd been sitting in this cubicle for nearly twenty minutes and the woman had scarcely been away from the phone. It seemed that everything else Ms. Anne Gilbert had scheduled was a good deal more important than Karen Fairgate. The guidance counselor had that vaguely superior air, as if being a housewife was in no way as important as having a *real* career.

"Oh, excuse me," Anne Gilbert repeated brusquely as she turned away to her intercom again. Just seconds before she had informed Karen that Michael should be suspended from school.

"Suspension?" Karen barely had the dreaded word out of her mouth when the other woman answered her phone yet another time. She stared at Ms. Gilbert in disbelief.

"Yes, suspension," Ms. Gilbert tossed back, almost blithely, and then became absorbed in her phone conversation, almost as if Karen had become invisible. "Hi, Sheila! Yes, so how are you?" Her face grew animated. "So, are we all set for tomorrow? Great!" She smiled. "Right, and I'll bring the back-up figures just in case the board isn't satisfied."

Karen shifted in her seat irritably, as the

guidance counselor droned on and on. In the outer room, Michael was on his feet again, playing carelessly with the pins on the cork bulletin board, pulling them free from the papers and allowing the sheets to fall to the floor in a pile. With a hopeless sigh, Karen turned away from this distressing sight, knowing that it would be useless to try to catch her son's eye. And it looked as if this incredibly inconsiderate woman was finally off the phone.

"Ah, what was I saying?" Ms. Gilbert turned back to Karen.

"We were discussing my son," Karen replied coldly, "and . . . suspension."

"Yes, well—" Anne Gilbert was obviously quite eager to make her point and bring this meeting to a close as soon as possible "—his behavior doesn't give us much choice."

Karen shook her head in protest. "But suspension? He's so young!" It simply wasn't right, not right at all. She looked at her child standing unhappily in the other room and her heart lurched.

Ms. Gilbert tapped the tip of her ballpoint pen on her desk with measured impatience. "There *is* an alternative," she replied. "We can forgo the disciplinary option if you let us put him in the special class for L.D.'s." Karen looked quite puzzled, and Ms. Gilbert had to resist an impulse to roll her eyes in a gesture of further impatience. "I'm talking about learning-disabled children, Mrs. Fairgate.''

Karen stared at the woman in shock. ''Michael? But I don't understand . . . he's so bright.''

Ms. Gilbert smiled stiffly. ''All parents think their children are bright.''

Damn that superior bitch, Karen thought with uncharacteristic savagery. Was the woman actually enjoying this? Karen knew her own reaction was not just the blind fury of a mother defending her young. She *knew* Michael, and she *knew* he was bright. Aloud, she said, ''Ms. Gilbert, I suggest you look at his testing scores. Go all the way back, and you'll see what I'm talking about.'' She noted the blank expression on the counselor's face, and the realization hit her at once. ''Wait a minute,'' she said, ''you *have* looked at my son's records, haven't you?'' There was an awkward pause. ''*Haven't* you?'' Karen tried to keep her voice from growing shrill. And once again, the telephone rang and Ms. Gilbert turned away, almost gratefully, to escape the heat of Karen's glare.

''Yes?'' she said into the phone. ''Very well. I'll look into it and get back to you.'' She ignored the dark, ominous expression on Karen Fairgate's face and started to laugh into the receiver. ''Did he say that? You're kidding!''

Karen watched her in disbelief and suppressed outrage. What would it take to get Anne Gilbert's undivided attention? How could any human being be so insensitive in a situation like this?

Ms. Gilbert hung up the telephone at long last, and sat up straight in her seat, as if to indicate that the discussion was over. "Think about the L.D. class, Mrs. Fairgate, all right?"

"That's *it?*" Karen half rose in her seat. Was she being dismissed as if this were some unsuccessful job interview? "What about my son's records? Are you going to look at them or not?"

Ms. Gilbert gave a tight nod. Why did parents have to be so argumentative? Why couldn't they listen to her advice? After all, *she* was the professional, not them. "I'll look at the records, but—" The buzzer rang again, and she reached for the telephone, only to be stopped by the hard grasp of Karen Fairgate's hand on her arm.

"You sent for me." Her tone was unrelenting. "You've made two suggestions . . . either suspension or a class for slow learners." Karen's voice had a razor's edge. "These are serious courses of action, Ms. Gilbert, and you haven't even looked at his records. Why, you don't even know my son! What gives you the right to make a decision like this so . . . so casually?"

The buzzer rang again, and Ms. Gilbert's eyes narrowed. "Let go of my arm," she commanded tautly.

Reluctantly, Karen released her grip on the guidance counselor's arm, but she did not retreat from her combative stance.

"Hold my calls," the other woman muttered into the intercom.

"Thank you," Karen said chillingly.

The guidance counselor made a production of shuffling the files on her desk. "I haven't looked at the records," she finally conceded. "I should have, and I will. But, whatever they say—" she tapped her fingernails on one of the folders "—we'll still have an unruly kid with a zero attention span who can't get along with the others and does lousy schoolwork."

She was fully aware that every single word pierced Karen like a sharp knife, but she was also far too annoyed with the other woman's aggressive attitude to make any attempt to soften the blow. Anyhow, it was time parents like Karen Fairgate accepted the truth about their kids. They simply weren't going to be nuclear physicists or brain surgeons.

"We don't make the kids, Mrs. Fairgate," she continued bluntly, "we work with what you send us." That was the truth and it simply had to be said, Anne Gilbert told herself. "I'm sorry. You come up with a suggestion that works, and we'll listen." She folded her hands on top of the desk in the usual gesture of the concluded discussion.

Karen took a long breath and slowly rose to her feet. She regarded Ms. Gilbert with cold eyes. "I will," she answered finally and turned to leave. Out in the hall, Michael stood waiting. Karen smiled at him lovingly and took his hand in hers. Together, they walked from the building. Yes, Karen thought silently, as she drove the car out of the visitors' parking area, there had to be a better answer. She gave Michael a concerned glance. She would think of an alternative.

Karen waited until after dinner to tell Sid. They were alone in the kitchen. "You heard me," she repeated to her husband as she continued to load the dishwasher with dirty plates and silverware.

"But suspend him?" Sid echoed in disbelief. "Don't you think that's a little severe?" He was hovering over the stove preparing fresh coffee.

"This was the third time this month I've been called down to the school." Karen leaned unhappily against the counter. "His grades are slipping, Sid. He's been fighting a lot and—" Her voice was suddenly drowned out by the whirring of the coffee grinder. She shot her husband a disapproving glance, and waited for him to turn off the appliance.

"If we've got a problem," Sid argued, "why am I hearing about it only now?"

"You're not!" Karen's voice was sharp. "I've mentioned all this before, and you live in this house, too. *You've* seen the way he's been behaving."

Sid shrugged and began to search for coffee filter papers. "He's been acting like a normal kid, honey." He scratched his head, somewhat perplexed. "Have you seen the filters?"

Karen gestured at the cabinet impatiently. "Sid, last night was *not* normal."

"I don't know," her husband replied, locating the package of filter papers and placing one inside the coffee maker. "Maybe there's too much pressure on him."

"What kind of pressure?"

Sid crossed his arms for a minute. "You know what I mean, Karen. Under pressure to get the best grades, and live up to Eric and Diana's example." He hesitated. "Maybe you ought to back off a little."

Karen's eyes widened. "*I* ought to back off?"

"Well—" Sid shrugged and poured a measured amount of cold water into the machine— "you know how you can be . . ."

The gauntlet had been thrown, and Karen set a stack of dirty plates down on the counter abruptly, taking several steps toward her husband. "How *I* can be sure beats neglecting him!" she snapped.

"And what is *that* supposed to mean?" Sid's retort was equally frosty.

"Look—" his wife threw up her hands in exasperation— "you're gone more than you're here. You leave early in the morning. You get home late. You even work weekends on that engine of yours."

"The car isn't the cause of Michael's problem," he stated tersely.

"Well, neither am I!" Karen shook her head defiantly. "It's just not that simple, Sid." She paused. "Michael's in trouble. I'd like him to see someone. A psychologist."

Sid did not reply right away. He stopped pouring the water and stared at Karen in disbelief. After a moment, he pressed his lips together tightly. "Let's not overdo it, Karen."

Karen was unmoved. She hated to argue with her husband, but their child's future was at stake. "I think he needs professional help, Sid," she replied quietly. "I really do."

Sid was adamant. "We don't have to hire a shrink to straighten out our son." He'd had an aversion to members of the psychiatric profession ever since childhood. But he could see how unhappy Karen was at his brusque response and felt like the world's cruelest bully. He hadn't meant to be so insensitive to her feeling. In a conciliatory tone, he said, "Look, honey, why don't we take him to the beach this weekend—you know, to that picnic everyone is going to—and I'll have a nice, long talk with him."

"Simple problem, simple solution, right, Sid?" Karen shot back bluntly.

Sid poured out a cup of fresh-brewed hot coffee for each of them and pushed one mug gently toward Karen. "It's worked on two kids so far. Why are you trying to make an exception with Michael?"

Karen ignored the coffee. "Because he *is* an exception! We've never had to deal with anything like this before, Sid." She sounded desperate, hopeless.

"Then let's deal with it right here" was his purposeful reply. "Right here, Karen. It couldn't hurt to try."

But Karen was at the end of her rope. "Okay, then *you* try!" she retorted sharply, and marched toward the living room, pausing in the doorway to deliver her parting shot. "If you gave him half the time you gave that engine—a quarter of the time, even—we'd all be better off." And with that, she flounced out of the room, feeling completely alone and alienated.

Chapter Eight

Some Listen, Some Don't

Sid looked up from the computer printout and shook his head at Gary. "There's no getting around it," he declared glumly, "these figures don't lie. We're losing money every time we service those cars we sold to Orchid Cab."

Gary fidgeted uneasily with the sleeve of his sports jacket. "It's the parts, Sid. Wholesale costs increase every month."

Sid pursed his lips. "And we promised them parts and labor for three years." Damn, why hadn't he followed his own gut instinct this time? Why had he given in to Gary on the Orchid Cab deal? Sid was more annoyed with himself than anyone else. He should have known better, having been in the business for nearly twenty-five years.

"I know about the deal," Gary muttered. "I made it, remember?"

Sid sighed. "Look, I'm not blaming you. Frankly, the warranty plan looked great on paper."

Gary glanced disparagingly at the printout. "Well, it doesn't look so hot on *this* paper."

Sid reached into the pocket of his coveralls for a walnut and chewed on it thoughtfully. "You're right about that, but the fact still remains that a deal's a deal. They've got every right to hold us to it."

Gary was uncomfortable. "Sure, but they're businessmen, too, and they like us. I think we ought to talk with them."

Just at that moment, Linda Striker, looking flushed and excited, knocked on the open door. "Am I interrupting something crucial?"

Sid shook his head. "That's all right. What's up?"

"The stress test just came back from the lab, and you won't believe it!"

Immediately, the problems with Orchid Cab and Delivery receded into the background, for here was news Sid Fairgate considered *really* important. News concerning his beloved engine. He shot up from his seat as if propelled by a rocket. "Let's have a look!" he exclaimed enthusiastically to the young woman mechanic. Gary couldn't help notice that Linda was blushing—two bright spots of pink on her smooth, pale cheeks.

So that's how the wind blows, he thought

to himself with amusement. *Old Sid had better watch himself*.

"Pursue this thing with Orchid if you want to, Gary," Sid called back over his shoulder, "but I think we're just going to have to end up eating crow *and* our losses."

Gary forced a broader grin than he truly felt. "I was raised on chicken, fried steak and catfish," he informed his partner, in a tone that resembled the bravado of his brother J.R. "Let me tell you, Sid, crow couldn't be all that bad!" Sid nodded and left the room with Linda. After a moment, the smile faded from Gary's face and was replaced by a worried frown.

Abby sat patiently behind the desk, listening as her older brother explained the bookkeeping system of Knots Landing Motors.

"You got that so far?" Sid asked. "After you tabulate the daily sales and expenses, you—"

"You post everything to the general ledger, then run your totals." She sighed and stretched out a long, silky-stockinged leg in front of her. "Sid, bookkeeping's bookkeeping. The same principles apply whether you're selling cars or catnip." She loved her brother dearly, but sometimes he could be such a stuffed shirt. It was nice of him to set her up on this job, though, and working for your own brother, you could probably get away with being late, Abby supposed with a secret smile. If only Sid didn't look so worried these days, she thought. She wondered what was eating him. Well, at least he didn't have to worry about the accounts at Knots Landing Motors any longer. Abby prided herself on her ability to pick up any skill, and she had always been a whiz with numbers. And even if working at a car dealership wasn't the most glamorous job in the world, it was the best she could manage right now, and besides—her vivid blue eyes caught a glimpse of Gary Ewing entering the office—this particular job might have some very pleasant fringe benefits.

"How's it going?" Gary glanced at Abby with his usual bright smile. Unlike Richard Avery, Gary Ewing never leered; in fact, there was almost something impersonal in his appreciation.

"I can't complain." Abby smiled her most dazzling smile and then delivered her never-fail playful pout. "Except that I've been here over an hour and still haven't had a coffee break."

"She hasn't tasted the coffee yet," Sid said and smiled in amusement.

"I smelled it on the way in." Abby continued to smile, very sweetly, in Gary's direction. "What this place needs is a woman's touch." She paused. "Sid said if I had any questions, to ask you, okay?"

"Sure, anytime," Gary responded vaguely. He turned to Sid. "Look, I want you to know that I've set up a lunch meeting with Frank and Roy."

"Why didn't you tell me before?" Sid asked in surprise. "I'll change and be with you in a second." He headed for the door, only to be stopped by Gary.

"Listen, Sid," he urged, "let me take care of this . . . alone."

"I don't understand . . . wouldn't it be better if both of us showed up?"

Gary shook his head quickly. "That's overkill. Believe me, I know these guys. They like me. I'll stroke them a little and see what happens." He waited expectantly for his partner's reply.

"All right." Sid nodded in assent, almost happy to be relieved of the problem.

Gary turned back to Abby. For the first time, he noticed how attractive that silk dress she was wearing looked on her slim frame. She would be a very delightful addition to the office, no doubt about that. "I meant what I said, Abby," he offered softly, "if you have any questions at all, don't hesitate to ask."

Abby smiled brightly. "I certainly won't."

Sid watched Gary leave the room, and suddenly he was worried. Was it such a good idea, after all, to send Gary alone to a meeting with Frank Korshak and Roy

Lance? Was he shifting too many of his own responsibilities onto his new partner? Maybe he ought to come along, anyhow, despite Gary's reticence. But, in the end, he decided against it.

"We appreciate your situation, Gary." Roy Lance poured himself and his partner another glass of wine.

Gary, knowing the dangers of even a single glass, refused again, insisting on another club soda. "I feel pretty ridiculous about the whole thing. I mean, Sid and I are willing to work with you guys any way we can. If you've got a suggestion . . ."

They had just finished lunch in the posh restaurant, and Frank Korshak lit up another one of his cigars. He glanced at Roy, who pulled out a briefcase. From one of the compartments, he drew out a thick computer printout and passed it over to Gary. "We'd like you to take a look at this." He watched as Gary examined the pages. "After you phoned us this morning about the problem, we made a few phone calls on our own . . . to various business associates, parts jobbers—"

"Wholesale parts," Frank emphasized in his gravelly voice.

Roy continued, "We explained your situation, pulled a few strings and came up with that parts inventory you're looking for."

Gary shook his head in wonderment.

"This is absolutely fantastic. If we had an inventory like this—"

"You do," Roy cut him off. "It's being put together for you right now."

Gary looked at the young man questioningly. Things were suddenly moving just a little too fast. "Wait a minute. I'm not sure we can afford . . ." he paused and waited for one of his two companions to name a price.

"Fifty grand?" Frank Korshak blew perfect smoke rings with his cigar.

Gary was stunned. Even at wholesale prices, the parts listed on the computer printout were worth at least three times that amount. "I don't get it," he stated, dumbfounded.

Roy smiled. "It's quite simple. You went out on a limb for us. You got your partner to go along with us on this deal. See it as our way of returning the favor."

Gary glanced over the inventory again, and another thought occurred to him. "Are these parts new . . . or used?"

"Reconditioned," Frank replied.

"But fully guaranteed by our associates," added Roy quickly.

Gary continued to consider the printout, and after another long moment set the thick stack down and smiled at the two men. This offer was just too tempting to pass up. "Fifty grand for the complete inventory?" he asked again.

Roy nodded and then inquired, "You'll

want to check this out with Sid first, I assume?''

"Sure, but it's just a formality," Gary answered hastily. He couldn't imagine his partner turning down a sweet deal like this. "I'm sure he's going to go for this."

"He'd be crazy not to," Frank Korshak remarked and gave a low laugh.

Gary watched, a little self-consciously, as the two men raised their wineglasses to him in a toast.

"Pleasure doing business with you, Gary," Roy said. "Here's to a long and enjoyable relationship."

Abby Cunningham sat quietly in the back seat of Gary Ewing's automobile, delighted to have finally solved the problem of transportation to work. The secret was to drive in with the bosses. In the front seat, however, all was not peace and tranquillity. Sid was intently leafing through the pages of the inventory printout that Roy Lance had given Gary yesterday. Abby knew her big brother well enough to sense the frown knitting his eyebrows together, even though she couldn't see his face from her seat. The car lurched at a traffic light suddenly, and all the personal effects that Abby carried with her almost went flying to the floor. Just barely, she managed to catch the giant philodendron before it collided with the front seat. Abby smiled in contentment. Even if things weren't smooth sailing between Gary and Sid, she still intended to enjoy herself at the new job—she had brought all her favorite pictures and office knickknacks, and intended to make life at Knots Landing Motors as comfortable as possible. At the same time, even though she acted uninterested in the conversation taking place in the front seat, she was as alert as a lion on guard at a cave.

"The Orchid Cab guys were amazing," Gary rambled on enthusiastically. "No hassles, no complaints, nothing. They just wanted to help."

"Why?" was Sid's monosyllabic reply.

Gary shrugged. "It's obvious, isn't it?"

"No," the other man responded curtly. "Why don't you enlighten me?"

"They appreciated the deal we made on those cars."

"Uh-huh."

"And they're just returning the favor." He hesitated. "It's good business, Sid." Gary tried to keep his eyes on the traffic ahead.

Sid didn't say anything for a moment, but disapproval was evident on his gaunt features as he set down the printout on the space between both men. "If we did business like this," he uttered at last, "we'd be *out* of business." He paused for emphasis. "Fast!"

Gary tilted his head questioningly. "What do you mean?"

"Do I have to spell it out?" Sid retorted. "What do you figure these parts are worth?"

Gary turned away evasively. "I'm not sure."

"You're not sure," Sid almost snorted. "A lot more than fifty thousand dollars—am I wrong?"

"Uh, that's difficult to say," Gary replied unconvincingly.

The muscle began to tense in Sid's jaw. "Well, if you can't say it, then *I* will. Anyone who's offering this kind of deal is either stupid or crooked." He almost glared at his partner. "I'm neither, but I'm not so sure about your buddies Frank and Roy."

Gary shook his head in mild annoyance. "Sid, come on. This is a hell of an opportunity." Inwardly, Gary had been rather surprised at the degree of his partner's reluctance to go for the Orchid deal. It had never occurred to him that Sid would make such a hassle over a damned good deal like this one. No wonder the guy never got anywhere. He stopped himself, realizing how unnecessarily harsh he was. Sid was successful enough in a small-town kind of way, but Gary Ewing couldn't help but measure success by his own family, back home in Dallas. Home, he thought bitterly. When the hell was he going to stop thinking of that infernal place as home? It hadn't been home for a long time and never would be again. J.R. had made sure of that. Even after all these years, Gary couldn't stop blaming his brother for his own misfortune. "It's a hell of an opportunity," he repeated, half aloud.

"Then let somebody else grab it up," Sid snapped back. "I don't want to do business with them!"

Gary sighed and made one last attempt to get through to his partner. "Sid," he urged gently, "it could make a big difference to us."

But as far as Sid Fairgate was concerned, the matter was closed. "I'm sorry, Gary. The answer is no." The car finally pulled into the parking lot of the dealership, and he opened the passenger door. "I'll see you inside." In another moment, he had stepped out of the vehicle and disappeared toward the building.

Gary shook his head in repressed fury and slammed his clenched fist against the dashboard of the car. "Damn it!" he muttered aloud. "We're running a business, not a Sunday school! When is he going to realize that?" Completely oblivious to Abby's presence, he shook his head again in mute frustration and climbed out of the car, slamming the door loudly behind him. Unnoticed, Abby Cunningham sat silently watchful. Gary Ewing, she thought, was a man who had the right ideas about being a successful businessman. He was a man who wasn't afraid to take chances. Abby liked what she had seen this morning. Yes, she was most favorably impressed with Gary Ewing. Perhaps coming to work at her brother's dealership was the smartest move she had ever made.

It had been a rough day at the office for Laura Avery. The least she had hoped for, on her return home, was a pleasant smile from her husband or a firm shoulder to lean on. Richard offered neither. He'd been completely distracted during dinner, and he scarcely spoke to her at all, except to ask for more sour cream for his baked potato. As soon as the meal was over, he had disappeared into the den to listen to his Walkman stereo. Laura was starting to feel more like a housekeeper than a wife, and it hurt her. She finished loading the last of the dishes into the machine and untied her apron. Then she walked slowly into the family room and regarded her husband for a long moment. He was oblivious to the world, with those headphones fastened over his ears. Patiently, Laura sat down on the floor cushions next to him and waited for him to notice her. But Richard either didn't seem to be aware of her presence or, more likely, was making a point of ignoring her. It was happening more and more lately—ever since she'd sold the Vandenbrooke house in the Palisades. She leaned over. "Richard?" Still there was no response. "Richard?" After the second time, she shook him. "Richard!"

With an expression of supreme annoyance, he slowly removed the headphones and stared at her coldly. "I hope this is worth interrupting Ravel for, Laura."

She shook her head in frustration. "I don't know if I can compete with one of the French masters."

"You probably can't," Richard retorted, almost like a recalcitrant child.

"I . . . I just thought we could talk." Laura could almost feel the tears from long weeks of tension between them starting to form in her eyes. She forced them back. "We never seem to talk anymore, Richard."

He threw down the magazine he had been reading and regarded her with disdain. "So, *talk*."

Laura bit her lip. "This isn't exactly what I had in mind."

Richard rolled his eyes impatiently. "Talk's talk, Laura. You want to talk, we'll talk." He paused. "So?"

Oh, forget it! she thought bitterly, seeing his cold expression. What was the point? You couldn't squeeze blood from a stone. If Richard felt like talking to anyone, it was probably Abby Cunningham. Sure, he probably had no end of things to say to *her!* She shook her head angrily and rushed from the room. Richard watched her leave, shrugged carelessly and replaced the headphones over his ears.

Sid watched his younger son with curiosity. Since his argument with Karen, he'd carefully considered everything she had said to him. Of course she was right. He didn't spend nearly enough time with the boy, but this would change. Starting right now. He watched as Michael pumped his basketball with air. For the first time, he noticed an unusual degree of ferociousness for such a simple activity. Almost as if the kid was angry at the ball. He had to suppress a laugh. ''So, son,'' he began tentatively, ''has basketball practice started yet?''

Michael merely nodded and continued intently on his task with the hand pump.

''So, you're playing guard again this year?'' Then Sid realized that Michael wasn't listening to a word he said. ''Michael?''

His son finally looked up. ''Huh?''

''About basketball . . . are you trying out for guard again?''

Michael looked distracted. ''Uh . . . I guess.''

''How about school?'' Sid was beginning to feel like a talk-show host with an inattentive guest. ''Of course, you've got to take care of that before sports, right?'' His son didn't respond, and Sid tried another tack. ''You're having some problems, huh?

At school, I mean." He waited, and at last Michael sighed and looked back at his father.

"Yeah." He fidgeted. "I'm trying, Dad, I really am, but there's so much to remember in class that it makes me bored. Pretty soon, I'm all confused." He began to bounce the basketball. "Then the teachers start treating me really weird, and the kids all laugh, and I feel lousy."

For a moment, Sid was at a loss for words. He wasn't used to Michael being so vulnerable, not in front of him. Usually, Karen was the one the kids turned to. He reached out tenderly to ruffle the boy's hair. "It must be tough for you, son."

Michael nodded quickly. "I hate it, Dad! I just want to be like everyone else and I know that I'm not!" He began to pound the ball furiously.

"Michael," Sid said slowly, "when I was your age, I had the same kind of problem. It seemed everybody else was into something like baseball or music, but not me. All I cared about was model cars and working on my brother's engine. The other kids thought I was a nut. They laughed at me, too."

He paused. Even after all these years, the memory of not belonging was still painful for him. "I tried being like everybody else, but that made me feel even worse. After a while, I decided just to be me." Sid smiled. "That worked pretty well, and I know it will work for you. Just be yourself, son. Don't try to be like everyone else, because you can't.''

He noticed that Michael wasn't listening anymore; his eyes hadn't remained on Sid during the entire speech. The boy couldn't be still.

''Son?'' Sid asked, waiting for a response of any kind. ''Did you hear what I said?''

But Michael was beyond listening to his father. He was jumping up and down, completely immersed in the task of dribbling the ball, around and around the room. Sid shook his head and watched him in silence.

Chapter Nine

Decisions, Decisions

On Saturday, the weather was everything Karen Fairgate could ask for. A vibrant, sunny day—perfect beach weather, custom-ordered for family picnics. Almost everyone in the cul-de-sac was there, enjoying sand and surf. Brian and Olivia Cunningham were throwing a Frisbee with Jason Avery. Even Richard and Laura were there, seated a bit apart from the others, soaking up the sun. Karen squinted beneath her oversized sunglasses, trying to figure out what had gotten into Richard these days. Every time she saw him, he was wearing one of those personal stereos on his head. Almost as if he was doing everything possible to shut out the rest of the world—especially Laura.

But she didn't want to worry on a fabulous afternoon at Knots Landing Beach. The air was filled with the aroma of numerous outdoor barbecues, and teenagers frolicked around the volleyball nets, so much a feature of southern California beaches. She stretched out luxuriously on the huge blanket she shared with Sid and Eric. It was so wonderful to have the entire family together on a day like this. The five of them rarely had the opportunity to share so leisurely a few hours in the soothing surroundings of a sandy white beach.

Happily, she reached for the picnic basket and began to unpack the sandwiches. "What the—" Karen stared, incredulous. Almost every sandwich she had carefully prepared and wrapped had been partially opened, and huge bites had been taken out of each one.

Eric looked at his mother. "I think Michael got into them on the way down here."

Karen was shocked. "Why didn't you stop him? Or say something?"

Eric shrugged uncomfortably. It was hard trying to be a loyal brother. "I figured he's been getting into enough trouble."

Sid sat up and pulled off his sunglasses. "It's only a couple of sandwiches, Karen."

But she wasn't listening. "And the cookies . . . and the fruit. Would you look at all this? He's taken bites out of everything!"

"I don't mind," her husband answered calmly.

Irritated, Karen thrust a half-eaten sandwich at him. "You don't mind? Well, that's just fine! Here's what's left of your ham and cheese—*bon appétit!*"

Just then, Michael came hurtling up alongside of them, sliding foot first into the blanket. Everywhere, sand scattered and flew.

"Hey!" Karen cried out. This was it, this was absolutely the last straw. No, she quickly told herself, she must remain calm. She wasn't going to allow a little incident like this to ruin a perfect day at the beach. She bit her lip and suppressed the angry words that hovered on them.

"Michael," Sid said with sudden firmness, "enough. Just calm down. You haven't stopped jumping around since we got here."

Michael vaguely listened to his father and continued to rock back and forth on his bare heels, digging them further into the moist sand. "When are we going to eat?"

Karen's eyes narrowed and focused back on the ravaged picnic hamper. "Eat? You want to know when we're going to eat? Not only did you just have breakfast at home, but you already went through our picnic like a piranha fish!"

Michael wasn't really listening to the chastening tone in his mother's voice. All he could think about was how incredibly hungry he was all of a sudden. "I'm really starving," he complained.

"Michael . . ." Karen began warningly.

"Hey," Sid interrupted quickly, "I thought we were all going to play some volleyball."

"All *right!*" Michael agreed instantly. Now, this was something he loved to do.

Sid tapped his older son on the arm. "Come on, Eric, let's get a game going."

Karen watched, with an audible sigh of relief, as her husband and both sons began to jog down the beach, assembling teams for a volleyball match. She almost felt as if she'd survived a minor squall. Still, she thought uneasily, gathering up the remaining picnic items, the worst was far from over. She knew it instinctively, and the knowledge was most disturbing.

Everyone, it seemed, had joined into the spirit of the volleyball game. Even Richard Avery, who'd been so reclusive lately, was persuaded by Michael into playing the game. On one side of the net were Sid, Richard, Laura, Michael and Olivia. On the other side stood Valene, Karen, Eric, Jason, Brian and Karl Russelman, a local doctor and good friend to everyone there. Michael Fairgate seemed so excited to be playing and was especially delighted that it was his turn to serve. Unfortunately, every attempt he made to set the ball sailing over the net ended up with the ball caught in the web. With each miss, the boy grew more and more irritated.

It was now the other side's turn to serve, and Valene Ewing smiled cheerfully as she prepared to lob a powerful one right over the net. "Okay, all you turkeys!" she declared brightly. "Get ready!" In one clean smash, the ball went sailing across to the other side, right to Laura Avery. Laura was an excellent volleyball player and was about to make a perfect return, when Michael came hurtling toward her.

"I got it! I got it!" he yelled, and crashed right into Laura. As a result, no one got it, and the point went to the other team.

At first, nobody was particularly concerned, but then his behavior became increasingly annoying. He was all over his side of the court like a spinning top, smashing into every player and ruining almost every return. When by sheer luck, his team scored a point, and Sid gestured for everyone to rotate, Michael bumped into everyone again, causing great confusion.

"Michael," Karen warned, "settle down. I mean it." The words were barely out of her mouth, when Michael lunged in front of Richard Avery, who was about to hit the ball in play, forcing the ball into the sand.

"Do you mind, Michael?" Richard said, finally losing his patience. "Stay in your spot. That one was right to me.''

Even Eric was beginning to notice some-thing was really wrong with his kid brother today. He seemed even more crazy than ever. ''Cool it!'' he whispered to him. ''For cryin' out loud, can't you see how angry everybody's getting? You want to ruin the game?''

But Michael wasn't listening. He was a human dynamo, ramming into anything that got in his way, almost in a wild frenzy to be the only one to hit the ball. Blindly, he smashed right into Olivia Cunningham, knocking her down into the sand.

That was just about enough, even for his patient father. ''Michael,'' his voice was pure steel. ''Get off the court.''

Even Eric was surprised at his father's icy rage. ''Dad, it was just an accident, I'm sure he didn't mean to—''

''I said, get off the court . . . *now!*''

''But, Dad—'' Michael protested, feeling terribly picked on all of a sudden.

Even Karen wanted to protest against her husband's sudden rage. ''Sid, it's only a volleyball game.''

But Sid waved her away with his hand, watching his niece crying where she had been shoved down into the sand. Val Ewing looked at the girl compassionately, and knelt down beside her. ''Hey, honey,'' she said, her voice gentle, ''it's okay.''

But Olivia glared at Michael from behind

tear-streaked eyes. "You big nerd!" she sniffled. "They told you to stop. They told you."

Michael glared back. "Shut up, Olivia. Shut your dumb mouth!"

"Michael!" Sid boomed, but his son turned his back to him and began to run away toward the ocean. With a quick glance at Karen, Sid went running off after him. "Michael!" he called out at the figure retreating rapidly down the beach. "Would you stop! Wait a minute!" he shouted, "I want to talk to you!" He felt a sudden burst of energy and gained speed. Finally, although quite breathless, he managed to catch up with the boy. He grabbed him by the shoulders and turned him around to face him. Before he could say another word, his son gave a quiet sob and buried his face against his shoulder.

"I tried to stop, Dad," he began to cry, "but I couldn't stop. I didn't want to hurt anybody. . . ."

Sid stared at his son in sheer astonishment. He had never realized the pain the boy was feeling. "Michael . . ." he said soothingly. There were no other words he could think of to say right now. The situation was far too overwhelming at the moment. All he could do was put his arms around his sobbing, unhappy child.

"What's wrong with me, Dad?" Michael whimpered in total misery. Right now, he felt like the biggest jerk in the world. Olivia was right when she called him a nerd. He was a nerd . . . the nerdiest kid who ever lived. "What's wrong with me, Dad?" he repeated tearfully.

"Shhh," Sid continued to hold his troubled son reassuringly. "There's nothing wrong with you, son. Nothing at all."

But even as Sid spoke the words, he knew he was lying, and that Karen had been right again. As he held the weeping child, he could make out the distant figure of Karen sitting on the blanket, watching them silently. They would have to do something; he realized that now. Something far more drastic than a simple picnic. But the question was, what to do? Where did they even begin to unravel Michael's bewildering problem?

Chapter Ten
The Wrong Answers

As Sid sat in the psychiatrist's office with Karen, he was sure they'd made a big mistake. Dr. Ronald Phillips looked distinguished enough, with graying hair, and enough diplomas on his paneled wall to impress most people, but Sid hadn't liked him from the first moment. There was something overly—what was the word—*curious* about the man. Oh, sure, shrinks were supposed to be curious, but this one almost seemed to savor discovering some dark hidden secret lurking in the Fairgate family attic. The doctor insisted there was no way he could begin to help Michael until he knew more about the two of *them*. He'd noted the way Phillips observed his and Karen's mutual discomfort and actually smiled slightly.

"Tell me," the doctor continued, "has there been much stress in the family recently?" He paused. "Anything unusual?" There was an awkward pause, and finally Sid found himself admitting that he'd been accused of attempted rape. He'd tried to forget that disastrous episode in his life: he had picked up a young hitchhiker who'd tried to extort money from him and then cried rape when he didn't pay. After weeks of torment, Sid was vindicated when the girl confessed to the D.A. It was a terrible chapter in his life, better left forgotten, but if the doctor thought it was necessary to be open and honest, well, it was all right with Sid. At first. Then he noticed something very odd. Every time he and Karen tried to bring the subject back to Michael, the doctor insisted on returning to the unfortunate episode of the rape trial.

"You should talk to your son about this," Dr. Phillips was insisting, "I'm sure he's still very upset."

"I talk to my son all the time," Sid said between clenched teeth.

"Hmm," the doctor took off his glasses and observed Sid shrewdly. "And how did this rape thing make *you* feel, Mr. Fairgate. You really should express your feelings."

Oh, to hell with this! Sid thought furiously. What a waste of time and a waste of sixty dollars an hour! "I don't have to come to some doctor to express my feelings."

"You agreed to do this to help Michael," Karen murmured underneath her breath.

Was Karen actually suckered in by this quack, Sid thought acidly? "This is so stupid!" he said to her. "I have no problem talking to Michael."

"No," Karen agreed coldly, "only *listening* to him!"

"Now wait a minute, please," Dr. Phillips intervened. "Let me ask you both: do you really want to be here?"

"No," Sid said at the precise instant when Karen said "yes." And so, it was checkmate.

"Maybe you ought to go home and think about it," Phillips announced. "I can't help you unless you want my help."

Karen looked helplessly at Sid. What were they going to do now? But her husband couldn't wait to get out of that oppressive office. He had definite ideas on what to do now.

The argument didn't last very long, as far as their arguments usually went. Sid was convinced that the best therapy for Michael was to spend an afternoon in the garage with his father. "You can help me work on the engine," he declared. "Would you like that, son?"

"Oh, wow, Dad!" Michael was beside himself with pleasure.

Just to see the look of delight on the boy's face warmed Sid's heart, but

Karen's reaction was another story. "You're taking him to the garage?" she inquired abruptly.

"An afternoon there is going to be worth six months in Dr. Phillips's office," he asserted.

"That's your solution to the problem?" Karen put her hands on her slender hips.

"Sure!" Sid retorted. "You heard him. He's happy, excited—"

"He's yelling," she cut in. "I hear it all the time."

"Karen," Sid warned, "I know you want to make a big deal out of this—"

"You bet I do," she tossed back. "You think it's as simple as changing a few spark plugs, but you're wrong! This goes deeper, and you're not even willing to admit there's a problem!" Karen's eyes flashed angrily. "Your mind was made up before we even went to Dr. Phillips."

Sid ran his hand through his hair. "That's not so, Karen. I went and I listened, but the fact is I'm simply not as impressed as you are by some diplomas on the wall."

Karen refused to let it rest. "You're just scared you're going to hear something you don't want to hear. About Michael. About *us*."

"Oh, so now there's something wrong with us. First it was Michael, then it was me, now . . ." Already, Sid didn't like the dangerous direction the argument had suddenly taken. He turned his back to her.

"Sid," Karen said, quiet but terse, "how can I get you to deal with this?" She inhaled deeply to keep her anger in check.

"I can tell you how," her husband answered brusquely. "You can let me deal with it in my own way! At least if I take him to the shop, he won't have to put up with this constant nagging." With that, he marched out of the room, furious.

Karen could only stare after him, feeling an odd combination of anger and sadness. Never had she felt so helpless.

So far, Michael was enjoying his day at Knots Landing Motors. His Aunt Abby was happy to see him, he noted, and so was that totally awesome lady mechanic, Linda. She was really helpful to him, too, showing him all around the garage. While Sid disappeared to find them both some overalls, Linda pointed out to Michael the special engine his dad was working on. To his untutored eyes, the engine he'd been hearing so much about recently didn't look particularly special at all. It just looked like any ordinary engine.

"Here's a set of overalls for you, son," Sid returned with a pair of large coveralls, which were way too large. Michael put them on and laughed. This was going to be fun, he thought. But then, slowly, he started to grow bored and restless. After a while it just wasn't all that exciting to watch his father and Linda hover over an engine and explain how the filthy thing worked.

". . . and this is the carburetor, right there," Sid was saying. "See those little things in there? The silver ones?"

But Michael was no longer listening. He was busy playing with a screwdriver. "When are we eating?" he wanted to know.

Sid groaned. "We ate lunch two hours ago."

"He's a growing boy, Sid," Linda smiled. "How about I make a hamburger run in a half-hour or so?" she asked Michael with a smile.

"Half an hour?" To Michael, that seemed like forever.

Sid gave an exasperated sigh. "Michael, do you want to learn something about engines or not?" But before his son could reply, Sid was being paged over the loudspeaker.

"I've got a call, son. Hang on, I'll be right back." He walked away to pick up the call, and Linda wandered off to her own work area, leaving Michael alone for the moment, while she searched for some tools.

Bored and restless, Michael began fiddling with the three hoses which hung down over the service bays. He pressed the first one, and discovered it contained air. He tried the second one and got water.

Impatiently, he grabbed the third one, which hung perilously close to Sid's engine, and aimed it right at the priceless piece of machinery.

"Michael!" Sid could see this happening from across the room. "Stop!" But the warning came too late. Michael pressed the nozzle carelessly, sending a huge glob of oil right into the engine. Furiously, Sid grabbed the hose from the terrified boy's hand.

"Dad, it's okay. I'll clean it up. . . . I'm really sorry!" He ran for the toolbox, and reached for the rag which dangled out of it. In the boy's frenzied haste, he knocked the box over, sending tools all over the floor. Continuing to panic, Michael ran headlong into a tray of nuts and bolts, spilling these all over the floor, too.

"Michael," Sid called after him, trying desperately to grab hold of the boy, "it's all right. We'll take care of it."

But Michael was oblivious. He'd made such an awful wreck of things, he thought miserably. Wasn't there anything he could do right? Just at that moment, he went sliding on the oil slick his carelessness had created, and his body went sprawling. Linda and Sid watched in mute horror as Michael's head hit the corner of the steel tool box. He lay there on the concrete floor, blood oozing from his head.

"Michael!" Sid cried out, gathering the boy in his arms. Hastily ordering Linda to call Karen, he carried the bleeding child to his car.

After Karen arrived at the hospital, white-faced and stunned, Dr. Karl Russelman took her and Sid aside and convinced them that the boy would be all right. There was nothing to worry about. Except for some minor contusions and a scalp wound, Karl insisted, Michael would be all right. They were taking him down to X-Ray merely as a precaution. "Oh, he'll have a headache for a couple of days," the young doctor declared, but that's about it. He's a tough kid."

"When can we see him?" Sid asked in a subdued voice, reaching for Karen's hand and clasping it tightly in his own larger one.

Karl smiled. "As soon as he's settled in his room. I'd like to keep him overnight, just to be safe." He hesitated. "You two got a minute? I'd like to talk about something."

A few moments later in the lounge, Karl said, "Sid, Karen's told me about Michael's erratic behavior. How did he act just before the accident?"

"Before he slipped, Michael was running around like he was possessed or something."

Karl nodded. "The way he acted when we were all playing volleyball at the beach on Saturday?"

"Exactly," Sid replied.

"Listen," Karl said tentatively, "since he's going to be here overnight anyway, would the two of you mind if I ran a few tests? Just some simple ones like blood, metabolism . . . strictly routine. Nothing that will hurt Michael, I assure you."

"Do you suspect something?" Sid inquired, noticing Karen grow tense.

Karl noticed the worry on their faces. "No," he replied quickly, ". . . a couple of ideas. I'd prefer not to say anything until I check it all out."

"Do it," Sid said assertively. "If there's something physically wrong with Michael, we must know." He felt his wife squeeze his hand in silent assent.

For Richard Avery, it was a triumphant return, worthy of a victorious Roman general, as he and L. B. Cargill walked through the offices of Pincus, Simpson and Lyle. Richard absorbed it all, down to the polite round of applause led by Simpson himself, and a cluster of secretaries, including Millie. Richard thought with deserved smugness that Arkansas Gas and Fuel had won its easement chiefly on the merits of his research. This morning, working together with Lynn Baker, Richard tasted the glory of success and it made him almost giddy. It was worth it to see the look on Simpson's face when Cargill gave Richard a congratulatory slap on the back

"They'll appeal, of course, but if I know Charlie Flagg, he'll have that pipeline built way ahead of that."

"I am very pleased," Simpson said, staring at Richard in a curious way, almost as if he were seeing the young attorney in an entirely different light.

"I'll let Richard fill you in on all the gory details," Cargill said. "He's certainly earned that pleasure. Meanwhile, I'm off to Arkansas first thing in the morning. This must be *au revoir*, gentlemen." He paused. "I'm sure we'll be working together again soon, Richard. Thank you." He headed toward the huge oak door.

Richard quirked his eyebrow. "I was hoping we could get together before you left."

Cargill nodded vaguely. "I'm staying on the boat. Give me a call."

After he left, Simpson turned to Richard and said ponderously, "Let's talk, Richard." He paused. "In the conference room."

Bewildered, Richard followed his boss down the hall, only hazily aware of Millie's encouraging wink. She obviously knew something, and Richard wondered what this was all about.

When they reached the conference room, Simpson shut the door behind them and offered Richard a cup of coffee. Richard found the senior partner's behavior bizarre, to say the least. Since when did

old man Simpson behave with such solici-
tude?

The older man drew a breath. "How
long have you been with us?" he enquired
pedantically, "Six years?"

"Nine," Richard answered coolly, feeling a vague insult.

"Well, well, as long as that!" Simpson
almost beamed. "You were a good soldier,
Richard. We never doubted that, but until
today we weren't sure you had . . . officer
potential."

Richard sat there calmly, understanding
full well what all this was leading up to.
"You never sent me into battle—" he
couldn't help but allow a tinge of bitter-
ness to escape "—I've been peeling pota-
toes and scrubbing latrines around here
since day one."

Simpson ignored the censure in the
younger man's voice. "Well," he proceeded, "we just might say you've earned
your stripes, as it were. How does Pincus,
Simpson, Lyle and Avery sound to you?"
He smiled at Richard magnanimously,
with the air of a monarch bestowing a
knighthood on one of his faithful subjects.

At least, that was the way Richard saw
it. A week ago, he would have jumped at
the opportunity Simpson was presenting
to him, but now he felt the bile rising in
his throat. He'd been at this penny-ante
firm since it was just Pincus and Simpson.
Into his embittered mind flew every injus-

tice, real and imagined, that the senior partners had subjected him to for nearly ten years. He'd never felt like part of the team at Pincus, Simpson and Lyle. He'd never felt liked by the other staff members of this stuffy law practice. They'd always acted so superior and condescending to him, and he could no longer contain the resentment that had been simmering in his stomach during all the time Pincus and Simpson had behaved toward him as if he were the lowliest lackey.

Common sense should have dictated to Richard Avery that this was a moment for discretion. Putting wounded pride aside, he should have been considering what a golden opportunity Simpson was offering him now. A partnership had been his dream for nearly ten years. But a deeper ambition had been sowed in the past week, and Richard's fickle heart soared to a higher ideal: a partnership with Lynn Baker Cargill. Sure, this was possible, he thought with renewed arrogance. Anything was possible for him now. He narrowed his eyes at the older man, who waited confidently for Richard's positive response. *Don't be so sure*, Richard thought harshly. Aloud, he said with unexpected curtness, "After nine years, you finally decide I'm good enough to be a partner?"

Simpson, who had never been spoken to by Richard in such a critical manner, was forced to confess, "We all make mistakes.

It took this case with Cargill to prove you're a better lawyer than I thought."

Richard rose to his feet. "I've been a better lawyer than you thought for almost ten years! If I lived in Beverly Hills or Brentwood instead of Knots Landing, you would have thought I was a better lawyer!" His skills had nothing to do with it, from his point of view. "I'm just a good lawyer, that's all. Better than you thought." His voice rose. "Better than *I* thought. And too good for Pincus, Simpson and Lyle!"

The other lawyer stared back at him, his mouth open in frank astonishment. "Am I to understand that you are declining my offer?"

He almost laughed into his ludicrous, Ivy League face. "You mean, do I quit? Yeah!" Richard was sitting on top of the world. "You *bet* I quit!" With an air of contempt, he inclined his head ever so slightly at his soon-to-be ex-boss and sailed from the conference room toward an even greater triumph.

Simpson stared at the door that closed behind Richard. A moment ago, he'd offered the man a partnership. Now, he was convinced that Avery must be totally off his rocker. He shook his graying head in disbelief.

Well, thought Laura, even if her personal life was a mess, at least business was going well. The three of them were sitting in Scooter's office—Scooter himself, Laura and Mrs. Otis Vandenbrooke. The wealthy woman from New England was expressing some degree of concern that there might not be enough room for a pool at the new home.

"Of course, I love the house," the woman insisted, "but the problem is space. I simply must have room to build an Olympic-sized pool for my husband. He's very particular about those morning swims."

Scooter, in his inimitable way, waved the problem away with both arms. "Believe me, Mrs. Vandenbrooke, there's room for a pool." He paused. "Where's that survey map, Laura?"

"It's right there on your desk, Scooter," Laura shot back with a smile, and then her smile faded. In the outer office she saw the most bizarre sight: her husband, grasping a bottle of champagne and dancing around the room. She blinked in horror and disbelief, as the strains of a popular Sinatra standard filtered into Scooter's office from Richard's booming basso.

"Chi-cago! Chi-cago! A toddlin' town . . ." he sang loudly and off key.

"Where did you say the map was?" inquired Scooter, for a moment unaware of the disturbance in the outer office.

"Right here." Laura reached over her employer's desk and plucked a large sheet of paper from the disorganized pile that was the rule rather than the exception when it came to Scooter Warren's desk top. Struggling to regain her lost poise, and desperately trying to forget that her husband stood only feet away making a complete fool of himself, Laura cleared her throat. "Now, about the space for that pool, Mrs. Vandenbrooke." She unfolded the map and held it in front of the dubious client. "Scooter is quite right about there being more than enough room."

"Chi-*cago!* Chi-*cago!* I'll show you around . . ." Richard's voice grew louder, and now Scooter turned his head in the direction of the outer office, alert and bewildered.

Richard was really making a scene. While trying to waltz with one of the secretaries he overturned a stack of coffee cups.

"Oh, no!" Laura groaned, as she saw him heading toward Scooter's office. She raced to the door, oblivious of the stares of Scooter and Mrs. Vandenbrooke. She had to stop Richard before he made a complete idiot of himself. Unfortunately, she was too late. Richard was already strolling in, with a grin from ear to ear.

"The town that Billy Sunday could not shut down!" he continued to sing loudly, stumbling straight into Scooter's massive oak desk. He saluted Mrs. Vandenbrooke and began handing out drinking cups.

"On State Street, that great street . . ."

Scooter rose to his feet and warned, "Richard, old friend . . ."

The other man ignored him and began to open the bottle of champagne. "I just wanna say, I just wanna say . . ."

Oh, God, Laura thought miserably, he's making a complete fool of himself . . . and me! Helplessly, she looked at Scooter and walked toward her husband. "Richard," she implored, "let's go outside." She placed a restraining hand on his arm, but Richard just shrugged it away and went on singing and struggling to uncork the champagne. "Please, Richard," she begged again.

"They do things they don't do in L.A.!" Richard belted out his play on the old lyrics with delight. With a final tug, he popped the cork at last, and champagne went spraying all over the office.

"Oh, God!" Laura was mortified. Richard just continued to sing, on and on, like some Las Vegas lounge singer. He didn't care, absolutely didn't give a damn, that he was humiliating her in front of Mrs. Vandenbrooke, her most important client, and Scooter, her boss. The latter two just stood there, numb with astonishment.

"Let's dance!" Richard sang out and grabbed Laura around the waist and began whirling her about the room. "We're Fred and Ginger!" he declared loudly, completely uncaring of the shocked stares of Mrs. Vandenbrooke and Scooter.

"Please, Richard!" Laura struggled in his grasp, almost on the verge of tears. "Stop it, for heaven's sake!" Richard stepped on her feet heavily, and Laura winced in agony. "Stop! Stop, already!" Her voice grew more hysterical. After a week of acting as if she was completely invisible, now he chose to play Fred Astaire in the middle of Scooter's office.

Richard began to whirl her around and around with even greater speed. She was a virtual prisoner in his strong grip, unable to break free. "Stop, Richard!" she cried out again, hoping she would finally wake up and realize it had all been some crazy, bad dream.

How Laura made it through that night, she never would know. Somehow, she and Scooter had managed to subdue a drunken Richard and place him inside her car. He was still singing exuberantly while she drove him home and led him up the stairs to the bedroom. In a few moments, though, he had fallen face down on the bed, giggling at some private joke, and passed out cold.

Now, with the digital clock reading only six in the morning, Laura sat up in bed and listened to the shower running. "Richard?" she called out. What was he doing awake at this hour? She padded into the bathroom, just in time to see him finish wrapping a towel around his lower body, and begin blow-drying his hair.

"Got a breakfast date with Cargill," he explained. "His plane leaves at eight-thirty, so I've got to rush."

Laura rubbed her eyes sleepily. "I don't understand—"

"I've got to iron out some last-minute details before he leaves." Richard parted his hair meticulously and held the brush by the dryer vent.

"Details?" Laura's eyes widened.

"Yeah," he replied indifferently. "The move, the house we'll need, school for Jason, you know." He paused. "And I think you should talk to Scooter about Chicago realtors. I'm sure he can recommend some good leads. After all, just because we're relocating in a new town doesn't mean you should give up your work, right?"

"No," Laura said coldly. She stood watching her husband.

"Hey," Richard said and gave a wave, "I'm sorry about yesterday. I guess I was a little overexuberant. You know how it is."

"No, I don't know how it is." Laura's simmering temper finally came to a full boil. "You humiliated me yesterday, in front of my boss, in front of a client—in front of my entire office. I was too angry to talk about this last night, and—" she paused "—you were too drunk to notice."

Richard didn't understand what she was so annoyed about. Hadn't he already apologized? "Look," he said and shrugged, "a little champagne never hurt anyone."

Laura bit her lip and walked back into the bedroom. What was the point? she thought unhappily. Richard could never admit he was wrong; it was simply against his nature. Sometimes, she wondered what made her love this man. "Have you discussed salary with Cargill?" she asked tightly.

Richard put on a fresh, white shirt and fastened his cuff links. "That's what we're meeting about. Of course, I'm sure it will be in the six-figure range."

His tone was so cocky that Laura asked, "Are you that sure?"

Richard glared at Laura with his usual impatience. "The thing I'm sure about is that I've been offered the opportunity of a lifetime. An opportunity to work side by side with one of the most prestigious attorneys in America—and all you can talk about is *money!*"

Once again, Laura found herself apologizing to her husband. "I'm sorry, Richard," she said quietly.

Richard thrust his arms into his suit jacket angrily. "You're not sorry at all! Who are you kidding, Laura? You don't want to go!" He stalked out of the room, slamming the door behind him. Laura continued to sit at her dressing table, shaking her head. How did he do it, every time? she wondered. But she had to admit that Richard was quite right about one thing. She didn't want to leave Knots Landing.

Chapter Eleven
Many Unhappy Returns

Richard arrived on the S.S. *Charlie's Rubber Ducky*, and was briskly informed by L. B. Cargill that he'd already missed breakfast, because Flagg had moved up his departure time. No apology, no regrets, nothing.

"About the job," Richard finally said, and was startled to discover that Cargill appeared quite bewildered.

"The job?" inquired the other lawyer.

"With you, in Chicago," Richard declared.

"Well," Cargill finally said and shrugged, "if you're serious about pulling up stakes, I'd be delighted to have you on my team, Richard." He paused. "What kind of money are we talking about?"

Richard shrugged expansively. "I was about to ask you the same question."

Cargill laughed and made some inaudible remark, then regarded the young lawyer for a long moment. "I'll start you out at twenty-eight five."

Richard stared at him in shock. Was he kidding? Was this some kind of a joke? Twenty-eight five? That was nearly ten thousand dollars less than he was already making at Pincus, Simpson and Lyle. *Was* making, he thought with a twinge of panic. "Mr. Cargill," he said, "I'm afraid you don't understand—I'm already making thirty-seven." He thought of the difficulty he was already having making ends meet, and the incredible expense of a move to Chicago was something else to consider.

But Cargill seemed unimpressed. The shrewd attorney knew he held the winning hand. "When you work for me, you're working for the best. Anyone I hire knows that, right from the start. That's how I get 'em for cheap." He gave Richard the full impact of his famous dark stare. "Now, if you're not willing to make that sacrifice—"

He was interrupted by Flagg's chauffeur, informing him that it was time to depart for the airport.

"Just a minute," he informed the man-servant.

Richard's world was spinning crazily around him. "But, Mr. Cargill," he pleaded, "Simpson offered me a full partnership yesterday and I turned him down."

Cargill looked at Richard almost contemptuously. "That doesn't leave you much room to negotiate, does it?"

"I've got a wife and a kid," Richard said dully. "You're offering me a salary that wouldn't support a first-year law student and you know it."

Cargill rose to his feet. "I don't have time to haggle, Richard," he announced in a voice that brooked no further arguments. "I've got a plane to catch. If you change your mind, just call my office in Chicago." He handed Richard his business card, picked up his sleek leather briefcase and walked off the yacht.

Richard watched him leave with a dumbstruck expression on his face. The entire sky came crashing down on him and all his dreams of glory. He shook his head again in disbelief, and it took every ounce of willpower not to be physically ill. He almost staggered toward the railing of the boat and looked out into the sea with unseeing eyes. It was over, everything was over. His ambitions and hopes shattered beyond any hope of resuscitation. And for the first time in his life, Richard could not blame anyone but himself. Not even Laura.

"It's okay, I'm telling you, it's okay!" Scooter was gently reassuring Laura as she sat glumly in his office, still humiliated by Richard's scene yesterday. "See this!" Her boss pointed almost gleefully at the survey

map. "Look at this champagne splotch!
It's on the *exact* spot where I was going to
show Mrs. Vandenbrooke she could put in
her pool!" He chortled, and Laura wanted
to join in, but suddenly, all she could do
was cry.

"What on earth?" Scooter gave her an
affectionate hug. "You want to tell me
what's wrong?" He paused in bafflement.
"Did you think I was going to fire you,
kid? Are you nuts?" He stroked her hair
gently, unable to believe how soft it felt
beneath his fingers. Immediately, he
cleared his mind of such dangerous
thoughts and remembered where he was.
"You're the best thing that ever happened
to me . . . I mean, to this office. You're a
natural at real estate!"

Laura managed a faint smile. She was
thinking what a sensitive and kind man
her boss was. She wished all men were
like him.

Scooter continued to try to cheer up
Laura. "*You* made the Vandenbrooke sale,
not me! You're going to be one helluva
success, and I'm giving you your own
office and a fifty-fifty split on commis-
sions." He waited for her enthusiastic
response and received none. "Laura,
what's the matter?"

She sighed painfully. "Richard quit his
job to work for some hotshot lawyer in
Chicago. We're moving."

"I can see how happy you are about it,"

Scooter observed sarcastically.

"What choice do I have?" Laura looked at her friend despairingly. "It's a great opportunity."

"For him" was Scooter's harsh reply. "But how about you?"

"Well," Laura answered unhappily, "do you suppose you can refer me to some real estate people in Chicago?"

"Sure." Scooter nodded glumly. "But we're talking about a much different market out there. It won't be easy for you, honey."

"I know," Laura agreed hopelessly, "I know."

"Okay, let's get right to the point," Karl Russelman said to Karen and Sid, as they sat in his office expectantly. "I'm pretty sure that Michael's hyperkinetic—hyperactive." He watched the stunned expression on his friends' faces. "It was difficult to spot at first because he's older than most kids are when they first exhibit the symptoms, but the tests are conclusive." He paused. "Do you know about hyperactivity?"

Karen shrugged tentatively. "It has to do with the metabolism, right?" Vaguely, she recalled conversations with other mothers and remembered things like kids unable to sleep and unable to stand still for too long.

Karl seemed to read her mind. "Hyperactive kids are overly energetic with incredibly short attention spans.'' He looked at them. ''What I must emphasize to both of you is this: it is not psychological; it's a *physical* disorder. You two should stop blaming yourselves.'' He paused. ''Or each other.''

Sid shifted uneasily in his chair. ''Okay, so what do we do about it?'' he asked.

''The first thing I'm going to do,'' Karl said and smiled, ''is send you to a specialist, the best man I know in the field.''

''I know that some people talk about prescribing drugs for hyperactivity,'' Karen said uncertainly. ''I'm not happy about that, Karl.''

''Neither am I,'' Sid agreed, taking Karen's hand. ''I don't like the idea of giving Michael drugs of any kind.''

Karl nodded. ''I agree with you completely, and so does the person I'm sending you to.'' He hesitated. ''The specialist is better equipped to deal with Michael than I am, but as a friend, let me give you some advice.'' He looked at Karen and Sid kindly. ''A lot of hyperkinetic kids grow out of it. Until they do, you deal with the symptoms. Changes in the diet help. But the main thing is, well . . .'' His voice trailed off.

''What would you do if Michael was your child?'' Sid asked quietly.

Karl sighed. ''I'd take all that incredible excessive energy that he has and rechannel it.''

"What do you mean?" Karen asked.

"Take that energy and guide him with it. Have him use it up and wear him out." He shook his head. "I'm not going to kid you two about this, it's going to be terribly hard. We're talking about using up an almost inexhaustible supply of energy every single day. You've got to think of anything that burns up that energy. Athletics. Exercise. Dancing. Anything and everything you can name, and I guarantee that Michael will come out of it better tuned and in far better shape than most people." He paused again. "The hard part is this: he can't do it alone; he's too easily distracted. For example, if he's going to run a few miles every day, someone's got to be right there, running along with him."

"I'll be with him." Karen stood up from her chair. She smiled at Sid and Karl. "I'll be right there beside Michael." Now that Karen knew what the problem was and how to make things better, there was no limit to how far she was willing to go.

It wasn't easy at first. Michael couldn't believe the weird dinner his parents brought up to the bedroom. One slice of bread and a crummy bowl of beef broth.

"Changing your diet is the first step of your treatment," said Sid.

Michael pressed his lips together. This part was going to be a real drag. "Dad,

I'm really sorry about all the stupid things—"

"You have nothing to be sorry about, son." Sid ruffled Michael's hair affectionately. "Remember what I told you today?" After bringing Michael home from the hospital, they'd held a family powwow. Sid and Karen explained about hyperactivity and what it meant. At least Michael realized now he wasn't a nerd, not really. Maybe things would get better.

"Let's play some cards." His older brother, Eric, walked into the room with a smile. Eric and Diana were part of the treatment, too. All of them were going to work with Michael and keep him active and interested.

Sid watched both sons with a strange contentment in his heart and picked up the dinner tray. "I just want you guys to know," he said before leaving the bedroom, "it's been a tough year for everyone around here. I haven't been around as much as I should be. So, do me a favor. Don't let me get away with it. You need me, say so. I'll be here. Okay?"

"Sure, Dad." Eric smiled and started to deal out the cards. Michael nodded in happy assent.

Alone in the kitchen, Karen watched Sid return with the empty food tray. "How is he?" she asked.

Sid nodded. "Pretty good, now that he

knows none of this is his fault."

"We should talk," Karen began.

"I know." Sid set down the tray on the counter.

Karen sighed. "We didn't handle this one well, did we?"

"I guess not," Sid agreed. "We were blaming each other."

"It scared me, Sid," she confessed. "Not just the way Michael was, but the way *we* were, you and I." Her mind went back to how it was all those years ago, when she'd first met Sid. They'd been an odd combination, with their extremely different personalities. Good-natured, streetwise Sid and blunt, overanalytical Karen. She'd thought that the combination of personalities would be wonderful for the kids. Exposing them to different viewpoints, different ways of thinking. But when all this happened, she began to doubt it. "I thought we were just the wrong combination for bringing up kids," she admitted. "I thought, it just couldn't work."

Sid reached over and touched his wife's cheek. "It *has* worked, honey. They're great kids and the hyperkinesia doesn't come from us."

"I know that now—but before Karl told us," she murmured, "I was so terrified about Michael. I knew we'd made mistakes with Eric and Diana, but Michael . . ." she paused. "I thought he was our masterpiece, and we'd learned from our mistakes with the two older ones. It really threw me for a loop, and then, the worst part was all those awful arguments between us."

"I know, baby, I know." Sid embraced her tenderly. "It was a pretty rough ride for both of us."

Karen accepted the embrace with renewed contentment. She had been so vulnerable, struck at the very essence of her being. She had begun to doubt everything about herself. "Way down deep, I was thinking that maybe you were right. Maybe the environment I'd created at home was too pressured, too frenetic. Maybe it was all *my* fault."

"Now you know it's not," Sid insisted gently.

"Yes," Karen agreed, "but I'd already made a pretty astounding discovery about myself. I'm not as sure about my beliefs and instincts as I thought I was." She pursed her lips. "For all my strengths, I was just about ready to throw in the towel."

"I'm glad you didn't," said her husband, stroking the hair back from her eyes with infinite tenderness. He looked at Karen, her eyes radiant, and realized that she was more beautiful at this moment than she had ever been. Her body felt so slim and warm next to his. Sid shook his head in wonder and kissed her on the lips. The desire stirred within him like a warm flame coming to life again.

Karen responded to the kiss by wrapping her arms around his neck and pressing herself against Sid's firm body. In a few minutes, they walked arm in arm toward the staircase.

"We'll work on this together," Sid was saying. "Michael will be fine. I'm sure of it."

"I know. I'm sure of it, too." She clasped Sid's hand tightly, and together they began to climb the stairs.

Richard pulled his car into the driveway, still in a dazed state. He couldn't believe the events of the morning. How could a person be sitting on top of the world one moment and plunge down to the depths of the bleakest hole the next? There was no way he could possibly accept Cargill's stingy offer, and returning to Pincus, Simpson and Lyle with his tail between his legs was absolutely out of the question now. Fool! he cursed himself. Simpson would never take him back now. Not in a million years. He was out in the cold. There was nothing at all. No choices. No options. Moving like an automaton, he walked from the car up the front lawn. He entertained the thought of drinking himself into oblivion, but dismissed that almost instantly. He was still hung over from the day before.

"Oh, Richard!" a sexy voice called out,

somewhere on the edges of his perception.

He turned around slowly to see Abby Cunningham, attired in the skimpiest little bikini he'd ever seen. It showed every luscious curve to absolute perfection. He regarded her silently and said nothing. He felt numb and unmoved.

"I waved," Abby said with her usual pout. "Didn't you see me?" Abby knew it was impossible *not* to have seen her. The bikini was a bonafide guarantee. Still, Richard seemed out of it this afternoon. He wasn't drooling over her as he should have been, and Abby was mystified.

"Sorry" was his uncharacteristically vague reply. "Guess my mind is somewhere else." His eyes didn't even seem to see her. Instead, he was practically staring right through her, toward some unseen horizon.

"Don't you like my new suit?" She continued to prod him. "It's called 'the ten.'"

"Real nice," he said briefly and turned away, toward the house.

Abby raised her eyebrows. Something really was wrong with this guy. "Hey, are you all right?"

"I had a rough day," he answered tonelessly.

Abby pursed her lips sweetly, up to the challenge. "How about a little tea and sympathy?" She took several steps closer. "Or maybe vodka and sympathy. I don't have to pick the kids up till three. You look like you need someone to talk to.''

Richard Avery had dreamed of an opportunity like this ever since Abby Cunningham had arrived at Knots Landing. But strangely, his appetite for such an exquisite promise of pleasure was gone. Completely. He felt hollow and very old all of a sudden. Almost dead inside. ''I'll take a rain check, okay? I've got a murderous headache.''

''Yeah, sure,'' Abby replied, completely nonplussed. ''That's what I used to tell my ex-husband.'' She smiled mischievously and winked, then flounced off toward her own house. Inside, she was incredibly annoyed. Usually, *she* was the person who did the rejecting. Abby did not care for set-downs of any kind, unless she was the person delivering them.

Richard watched her go, amazed at his own lack of reaction.

Despite the sumptuous meal Laura had so painstakingly prepared, Richard scarcely ate a bite. Laura could only watch him in puzzlement. Even Jason couldn't understand why his father looked so glum and wasn't laughing at any of his cool jokes. Richard tried to lose himself in a game of Ping-Pong later that evening, but nothing could allay the heaviness that covered his spirit like a dark blanket.

At bedtime, Laura put on her nightgown and gazed at Richard doing sit-ups on the bedroom rug. "We've got to talk," she said.

Richard ignored her, continuing to expend an extraordinary amount of energy on his sit-ups—far more than he ever had before.

"Why are you so mad at me? I don't understand . . ." Laura threw up her hands in despair.

"What do you want to talk about?" muttered Richard in a monotone, as he continued the series of repetitions.

"The job. Your job. My job. Us."

Richard shrugged. "So talk." He went back to his exercising.

Laura had had just about all she could stand. "Stop it! Stop right now and listen to me, dammit!"

Astonished at her tone, Richard sat up and stared at Laura.

She was shaking a bit. "I was thinking that maybe we could wait a few months before making the move to Chicago. Scooter says that I can be a real success, but I should wait until I've gotten my license before I pull up stakes here. I'm happy and proud for you, Richard, really I am. You've waited a long time for it. But the truth is, I've been waiting a long time, too, for something that makes *me* feel proud." She paused. "I know you'll be making enough money so that I won't *have* to work anymore, but I *want* to work." She knew that things could never go back to being the way they were before. Laura didn't want them to, either. She wouldn't feel good about herself, and she'd end up resenting both Richard and Jason. "All I need is some more time to prepare," she pleaded with him, "just a few months. That's not unreasonable, is it? Call Mr. Cargill. Please. Talk to him."

Richard took a deep breath. "I already have."

"Yes, but—"

"You don't understand, Laura," he said. "I turned him down."

Laura's eyebrows shot up. "You what? Why?"

Richard twisted his mouth. "I gave the matter a great deal of thought as I was driving over to see him, and I came to the realization that I was being unfair to you and Jason." He rubbed his moist hands on his sweatpants. "I didn't want to be so selfish. After all, we have a life here. It's true that I've always been frustrated in my job, but that's because I never dared to look for something better." He stretched purposefully. "That's what I'm going to do now, though. And we're not moving to Chicago."

Laura was completely dumbstruck. "Are you sure, honey?" she asked quietly.

"Quite sure. It will work out best for all of us," Richard uttered before joining Laura in the large, comfortable bed.

Laura watched her husband silently and

then leaned over and kissed him on the cheek. Unable to hold back her emotions, she kissed him again until he finally began to respond. This was what she wanted and needed—being close to Richard, being held by Richard. This was the way it used to be before all the terrible misunderstandings, before all the hateful arguments and thoughtless actions.

Richard was taking the lead now, pulling the straps down from Laura's nightgown and burying his lips against the creamy skin of her shoulder. Laura shut her eyes with happiness. He felt so good against her, his lips so warm and gentle. *The way it used to be.* Suddenly, she felt something else. Something troubling. In disbelief, she realized that her husband was crying. Actually crying, against her shoulder.

"Richard?" she whispered in a stunned voice. But there was no reply. He just continued to sob, in the very softest of whimpers. It was the crying of a child, an unhappy child who had lost all hope.

"Richard?" she asked softly again, and then understood that he would say no words tonight. Whatever pain was eating at Richard, he could not discuss it now. She held him tightly, like a mother holding a baby, and shook her head. Long into the night, he remained cradled in his wife's arms, his sobs ceasing only when he drifted off to a mercifully dreamless sleep.